Him and Her

A Story About Survival in the Arctic

Printed in the United States

Publisher: Mercer Publications & Ministries, Inc.

Stanwood, Michigan, USA

ISBN 13: 978-1-62329-065-8

ISBN 10: 1-62329-065-1

Acknowledgements:

Drawings by Olivia Kinsey

Cover pictures by iStock.com, Shutterstock.com

Design by Dorothy May Mercer

My sincere thanks to my wife, family and friends for invaluable help and encouragement.

TABLE of CONTENTS

Him and Her

A Story About Survival in the Arctic

Chapter 1 Deserted

Who they were, or why they wanted them dead, really didn't matter, now. The fact was they were leaving, and they wouldn't be coming back. There was no reason to. There was no way two people could survive on an Arctic island with nothing but the clothes they were wearing. It was late September, and it had been warm in Chicago when they were forced into the plane. In the far northern Arctic the sun would soon set for the winter. It was already getting close to freezing.

As they watched the plane disappear into the distance, he glanced over at her and saw the look of total despair on her face. It was understandable since they had no hope of surviving more than a few hours. They would probably freeze to death, and even if that did not happen, they had no food. Even if they had food, there was no way off the island. Their situation was indeed desperate.

If he had not been so intrigued with the Arctic, they probably would have been shot on the spot as had other people who were a threat to the boss. He had a very sadistic sense of humor. His enemies frequently died in a manner consistent with their area of interest. But none of that mattered now. They were there, and they would almost certainly die there. He could imagine the boss chuckling to himself as he thought about their demise.

He tried to think of something he could say that would encourage her. What could he say? They had no hope. Then a thought occurred to him. The Eskimos survived. Actually, that was about all they could do, but they did survive. If the Eskimos could survive, maybe they could too. However, the Eskimos probably brought something with them to the Arctic. They had nothing. The Eskimos also had dogs. They did not. Dogs were very important for survival in the Arctic. Then there was the danger from polar bears and wolves. Still there might be a chance, and he was not the type to give up without trying.

He felt like he had to say something. She looked so pathetic. "Well," he said. "It looks like we have a bit of a problem." At first she made no response. She was in a daze. Then she slowly turned toward him. It finally dawned on her what he had said. Her mental state was somewhere between desperation and hysteria. He didn't know what reaction to expect, but he didn't have long to wait before he found out.

In anger she lashed out at the only one she could. "A bit of a problem?" she said. "You fool; don't you know we will be dead in a few hours?" How could he respond? He wanted to comfort her, but there was no denying the truth of what she was saying. Still he had to try. "That certainly is quite likely," he said. That didn't come out well. She replied with even greater anger. "It isn't likely; it is certain. We will be frozen solid in a few hours, and no one will ever know what happened to us except the boss and his henchmen."

He had to think of something to say that would make their situation seem less horrible. "Well, that is one advantage anyway," he stated with a pitiful laugh. She was now totally irate. "How is freezing to death an advantage?" she asked with fire in her eyes.

He knew her anger was not really entirely directed at him, but she probably could say he was at least partly responsible for their situation. At least her anger would increase her adrenaline and help her stay warm and keep fighting.

Chapter 2 Surviving the Night

She had asked a question. That was good. It would distract her from dwelling on the hopelessness of their situation. Inactivity was the worst thing because it would cause them to freeze more quickly. If he could engage her in conversation, it would keep her animated, and maybe he could think of a way to keep from freezing.

He started, "If a person is going to die, freezing is one of the best ways. He feels cold at first and begins to shiver. The extremities become numb. Then he becomes lethargic and experiences amnesia. Finally he loses consciousness. At that point he could be revived if there was some way to warm him up again. One man was revived after his body temperature fell to 56.7 degrees Fahrenheit. Of course, if he can't be warmed again, his heart will stop."

This clearly did not comfort her. "Well, no one is going to warm us up again after we lose consciousness. We are going to die, and there is nothing anyone can do about it. Can't you get that through your head?" she raged.

"Well, that is another advantage we have," he replied.

"How is the certainty of our deaths an advantage?" she wanted to know.

"Isn't it obvious?" he said. "Because there is no hope of survival, they won't come back to check on us. That is one danger we don't have to worry about. "

"I think your brain is already becoming numb," she said in disbelief.

"Actually, there is another reason the hopelessness of our situation is an advantage. Since we have no hope, we have nothing to lose by trying anything we can think of to stay alive," he said with feigned cheerfulness.

"Oh, great! We have nothing but one advantage after another. We must be the luckiest people in the world," she responded sarcastically. "I suppose next you will tell me there is a gourmet meal waiting for us on the other side of that pile of rocks. Do we have a whole crew of servants to wait on us too?"

She was certainly animated. Wait. What had she just said? There was a pile of rocks. That was it. They could build a shelter. Now he saw a ray of hope. He jumped at the chance. "That's a great idea," he said. "We could build an igloo."

"There isn't any snow," she said. "How can we build an igloo without snow?"

"We only need snow for a snow igloo," he answered.

"I thought an igloo was snow," she said.

"Normally we think of an igloo as being made of snow, but the word actually means a house. It can also be made of sod, stone or wood," he informed her.

"I don't see any wood or sod," she replied.

"Well, there you have it. Since stone is our only option, that is what we will use," he said with satisfaction. "Besides, there are no trees on any of the Arctic islands unless you count the Arctic willow."

"Maybe we could cut down some Arctic willows and build a house," she suggested.

He laughed, "We can't cut down Arctic willows."

"Why not?" she wanted to know. "Is it against the law, or is it because we don't have an ax?"

"We can't cut them down because they are already down," he said with obvious amusement.

"What is so funny? Why are they already down?" she wanted to know.

"They are less than six inches tall," he said.

"I thought you said they are trees," she responded with irritation in her voice.

"They are," he replied.

"A plant that is less than six inches tall is not a tree," she insisted.

"Yes it is. It is a woody plant that lives for many years. One in Greenland was determined to be 236 years old. Height doesn't determine whether or not a plant is a tree. Do you think bananas grow on trees?" he asked.

"Of course," she answered.

"No, a banana plant is considered a perennial herb. It is not woody," he informed her.

"I don't care if you call it a tree or an herb. There are no bananas here, and I am freezing. If you think you can build a house or an igloo or whatever you want to call it, let's get started," she said.

With this he was in complete agreement. At least, the effort of moving rocks would help them stay warm, and it would keep their minds off the peril of their situation. As they tried to find rocks that were suitable to form a rough shelter, he attempted to keep a conversation going. "The Eskimos could build a snow igloo in one to two hours. It will probably take us longer because we are not as experienced, and we are using rocks. At least, we don't have to worry about the igloo melting when the temperatures get above freezing," he said.

"I suppose you are going to tell me that is another of our big advantages," she responded with more sarcasm. "Shall we build the servants' quarters now or wait until tomorrow?" At least, she was considering the possibility that there might be a tomorrow.

He needed to keep her talking. "I think tomorrow would be fine, and we can wait on the garage until we get a car."

Finally, he got a little laugh from her. It wasn't much, but it was something. As they worked, he kept her talking. It was mostly small talk. His mind was not mainly on the conversation or the construction. The shelter would help some, but it would not be sufficient by itself. They would still freeze. What they really needed was animal skins like the Eskimos used, but they didn't have any. What could he use for insulation? Whatever it was, it would have to be something from their environment because that was all they had to choose from. He looked around. The whole area looked very desolate. It was nothing but a bunch of rocks in the middle of an endless sea. If only something grew there. Then he remembered that something did grow on the Arctic islands. There were mosses and lichens. Maybe they could find enough to plug the gaps between the rocks. That would help some.

They were getting tired from moving rocks. He suggested that they take a short break from their work to explore the island. It was not very big. They could walk all the way around it in less than twenty minutes. She didn't see much point to the walk. There was nothing to see but rocks and water, but she welcomed the break. As they walked, he kept her engaged in talk. He didn't mention that he was looking for any type of vegetation. He didn't want to get her hopes up if there was nothing to be found. Then on a south-facing slope he saw what he was looking for. There were lichens. He acted like he had come across them by accident. "Look," he said. "There are some lichens."

"You saw something you like?" she asked.

"No, I said there are some lichens," he answered. "Lichens are plants that can grow in almost any environment. They cover about six percent of the earth."

"What can we do with them?" she asked.

"I thought we might be able to use them for the gaps in our shelter. Maybe they could provide some insulation. Let's see if we can scrape some off the stones," he suggested. They came closer. He found a rock with a sharp edge that he could use as a tool and tried scraping off some lichens. It worked. She found another small rock and proceeded to scrape as well. They soon had a pile of lichens. Then he noticed some mosses nearby. They might work even better.

The next question was how they would transport them to their crude shelter. He put some of them into his pockets. When his pockets were full, he stuffed some into his shirt. Then it occurred to him. Why not stuff all his clothes full of mosses and lichens? It would be like wearing a coat. That was the solution to their immediate problem. It would keep them from freezing at least for the night. He shared his idea with her, and she followed his example. Maybe they could survive for a while.

They returned to their new home and continued with the construction. If they could foil the boss's plan to kill them for just one day, it would be some accomplishment. They worked late to get the structure enclosed. It was very crude, but it served its purpose. They survived the night.

Figure 1 Building a Shelter of Rocks

Chapter 3 Freeze or Starve

Since they were able to survive one night, they could probably survive another. If they could survive two nights, why not three? How long could they keep from freezing? It was only late September. Temperatures would continue to go down for another three or four months. There was still a good chance that they would freeze to death, but they could probably last a month or so.

If they did stay alive that long, the next problem was how they would keep from starving to death. Even before they died from lack of food, they would die of thirst. Then there were all the other dangers in the Arctic. He was still pondering their dilemma when she woke up.

"Are we still alive?" she asked. Of course, the fact that she was able to ask the question provided the answer.

He tried to seem cheerful. "We are indeed. For the Eskimos, survival equaled success. Since we are alive, we are successful."

She was not at all cheerful. "I don't feel very successful. I just feel cold. I'm also thirsty. If we are not going to freeze to death, I am going to the shore to get a drink. At least we have lots of water."

"We can't drink the water," he informed her.

"Why not?" she wanted to know. "Are there too many germs in it?"

"We can't drink it because it is saltwater," he replied.

"How do you know it is saltwater? Did you taste it?" she asked.

"I know it is saltwater because it is the Arctic Ocean," he answered.

"But how do you know it is the Arctic Ocean? How can we tell where we are?"

He proceeded with his explanation. "We were in Chicago. I watched the compass on the plane. It showed that we were heading north through most of our flight. That means we were flying over Canada. Near the end we were over water. We did not pass over permanent ice pack, which means we did not cross the North Pole. That means we are on an island somewhere in the Canadian Arctic."

Here she intervened. "I watched the compass too. Near the end of the flight we were heading west. Maybe we are near Alaska."

He explained, "The reason the compass showed that we were going west is because it points toward the North Magnetic Pole. The North Magnetic Pole moves around. It is currently between Ellesmere Island and Greenland."

"Okay, are we on Ellesmere Island?" she wanted to know.

"Definitely not. Ellesmere Island is the tenth largest island in the world. It is over 500 miles long and has an area of nearly 76,000 square miles. It would be nice if it were Ellesmere Island because there are people there."

"How many?" she asked.

"About a hundred fifty," he answered. "Most of them live at a settlement known as Grise Fiord."

Next she wanted to know, "Are there other islands in the Canadian Arctic that are inhabited?"

"Oh yes. Baffin Island has a population of about eleven thousand. It is the largest island in Canada and the fifth largest in the world. Victoria Island is the world's eighth largest island, and it has nearly two thousand people. There are other smaller islands that are also inhabited."

"How many islands are there in the Canadian Arctic?" she asked.

"Between thirty-six and thirty-seven thousand."

"Wow! If there are so many, why can't I see any of them?" she wondered.

"That's easy to explain. They are spread out over an area of more than half a million square miles."

She thought for a few minutes. They had survived one night, and there were many islands around them even though they couldn't see them. If there were people on some of those islands, maybe their situation was not totally hopeless. Could they get to an inhabited island? For the first time she saw a dim ray of hope.

"Do you think we could get to Ellesmere Island or that baffling island you talked about?" she asked.

He replied, "It is called Baffin Island. It would be nice if we could get to one of them, but we don't know for sure exactly where we are in the Canadian Arctic. I think Ellesmere Island and Baffin Island are east of us, and Victoria Island is west of us, but I can't be sure. If we guessed wrong, we could end up in Baffin Bay or some other large body of water. I think a better idea would be to head south. We would eventually reach the Canadian mainland if we didn't find another island first. Of course, we can't go anywhere now because we don't have a kayak or an umiak."

"What is an umiak?" she asked.

"It is a large open boat made of skins stretched over a wood frame. All the Eskimos from Siberia to Greenland used them for transportation and to hunt whales and walruses," he answered.

"I thought you said there wasn't any wood in the Arctic," she objected.

"I said there are no trees on any of the Arctic islands. There are trees on the Arctic mainland south of the tundra. Sometimes there is driftwood that makes its way to the islands," he explained.

"Do you think we could find some driftwood for a fire? I'm cold," she said.

"Wood is much too valuable in the Arctic to use it for fire. Normally the native people used seal oil lamps for heat and light. Of course, we don't have any seal oil, and we don't have any way to start a fire," he replied. As soon as he said that, he realized that he was removing what little hope she had.

"So we can't drink the water, we don't have any food, we can't start a fire and we have no way off the island. Are there any other "advantages" that you want to tell me about?" she asked in frustration.

He tried to think of what to say. Things certainly did look grim. Then he realized that what she had just said did in fact specify the challenges they needed to overcome in precisely the order in which they needed to address them. Again he tried to be encouraging. "That is very perceptive. You have just outlined exactly what we need to do," he said.

"I did?" She was confused. "I thought I was pointing out problems, not solutions."

"Yes, indeed. I can see that you are going to be a big help in getting back to civilization." He didn't believe what he was saying.

She responded with hesitation, "Okay, can you explain to me how I have just solved all our problems?"

He tried to be careful how he answered. "Well, as you indicated, since we can probably keep from freezing for a while, our next most pressing need is to find something to drink." He hoped that would sound encouraging, but his scheme didn't work.

She replied, "Well, Mr. Smarty-pants, as you already pointed out, we can't drink the water."

"I said we can't drink the ocean water," he reminded her.

Again she resorted to sarcasm. "Oh, yeah, we just can't drink the ocean water. All we have to do is go to the drinking fountain. So where is it if you are so smart?"

There obviously was no drinking fountain, but her question was pertinent in its essence. Where could they get water they could drink? Precipitation, whether rain or snow, was fresh water, and even though there is little of either in the Arctic, because of the low temperatures it didn't evaporate very quickly. Maybe there was some on the island. Again he tried to sound positive. "You've made another good point. Let's see if there is any water on the island."

They had walked around most of the perimeter of the island, but they had not yet explored much of the interior. Perhaps there was a depression that had held some water or ice from the last rain. It would probably be ice now since the temperatures had fallen well below freezing during the night. They had only gone a short distance when they came across a small pool of water in a low area near the shore.

"Oh look," she said. "We are in luck. There is some water. Let's get a drink."

"Wait," he replied. "You can't drink that water."

"Why not?"

"It's saltwater," he answered.

"Now wait a minute. You can't possibly know that it is saltwater when you haven't even tasted it yet," she said.

"If you don't believe me, then taste it, but don't drink very much. It will make you sick."

She took his suggestion and went to the pool. After a small sip, she stopped. "Okay, so it is salty. I don't understand. How did you know?"

"That's simple," he said. "It's liquid."

"Water is supposed to be liquid, Silly," she objected.

"It is liquid when it is above freezing," he explained.

"Well then, it must be above freezing because it is liquid. It doesn't seem like it though," she said.

"It's not," he replied. "My guess is that it is around twenty-five to thirty degrees."

She felt like he was playing games with her. "But you said it would only be liquid if it were above freezing. You are contradicting yourself."

"Fresh water freezes at thirty-two degrees. Concentrated saltwater doesn't freeze until it gets down to about zero. In fact, that is why Fahrenheit started his temperature scale at the point he did. Freezing saltwater was the lowest temperature he could achieve. Ocean water has about 3.5 percent salt. That is why it freezes at around twenty- eight degrees." he explained.

Once again she felt discouraged. She was thirsty, and she had hoped for a drink. Would all the water on the island be salty? He knew what she must be thinking.

"This water is in a low area near the shore. It probably came from waves that came ashore when there was more wind. Let's look farther inland at a higher elevation," he suggested.

They did just that, and after a short time they came across a depression with some ice in it. They broke the ice and found that there was water under it. Now they knew they wouldn't die of thirst.

Chapter 4 Stop Staring

They both took a drink and felt somewhat refreshed. Then they sat down on the rocks to think of their next move. It was obvious that the greatest challenge facing them now was food. There was simply nothing to eat on the island. What could they do? He tried to think of a solution. Again he asked himself what the Eskimos did for food. In the books he had read it said that they had a nearly one hundred percent meat diet. On the mainland they depended greatly on the caribou, but there were no caribou on the island. There were musk oxen on some of the Arctic islands, but there were none here.

Then he remembered that the Eskimos normally lived near the shore of the Arctic Ocean because the sea provided much of their diet. There are about 240 species of fish in the Arctic and some, such as the Arctic cod, live throughout the entire Arctic Ocean. That meant that there had to be some near their island. The question was how to catch them. They didn't have a fishing pole or spear. If they had a net, maybe they could catch some fish. But they didn't have a net. Was there a way to make one? What could they make it with? He knew the natives had to use everything in their environment to survive. What did they have that they could use to make a net? There was water, stones, lichens and mosses. The options were very few, and none of them could be used to make a net. What could he do? He looked over at her. If only she could do something to help. Then it occurred to him that she could. He looked at her as he thought about his plan.

"Will you stop staring at me? I had enough of that at the restaurant." She was clearly annoyed.

He responded, "I'm not staring at you. I'm looking at your hair."

She was irritated. "Well, I'm sorry I didn't make it to the beauty parlor before we were so graciously invited to go on this little vacation." Sarcasm seemed to be her escape mechanism.

"We need something to eat," he said.

"You want to eat my hair?" she asked in disbelief.

"I don't want to eat your hair. I want to use your hair to get something to eat," he said. He forgot that she didn't know what he had been thinking about.

"We can't exactly take my hair to the market and trade it for food," she pointed out.

He needed to explain his plan. "I was thinking that maybe we could make a net to catch some fish."

She responded, "I never heard of anyone using hair to make a fish net."

"Neither have I, but I don't see why it couldn't be done. We have to use everything we have in order to survive."

She thought about his suggestion. It might work, and they really didn't have many options. "Okay," she said. "Maybe it is worth a try, but we don't have any scissors."

"Sure we do," he said. "Most primitive people used stones for nearly all their tools, and one thing we have lots of is stones."

That was it. They had a plan of action. The previous day they had used a sharp rock to scrape lichens off the rocks. Now they found other rocks that they were able to use to cut off some of her hair. A good pair of scissors would have worked better, but they managed to get the job done. Then there was the matter of how to form a net. They had no experience, but they thought that by braiding several strands together, they might be strong enough. It took several hours to make the net. By mid-day they were ready to give it a try. Where should they try fishing? It would have been nice to have a boat, but that was not an option. They walked around the island and finally found a spot where some rocks protruded out into the water. It was deep there, and they decided to try their hand at fishing. They spent the whole rest of the day there without catching anything.

She was hungry and discouraged, but he tried to comfort her. They had not caught anything, but they did see some fish. That meant that they did have a chance of catching something eventually. They would keep trying. What else could they do?

When it got too dark to continue, they returned to their shelter. It was very crude, but now it was their home. They had survived one night, and they had found water. They still didn't have anything to eat, but they had hope. Maybe if they could keep from freezing for another night, tomorrow they might catch a fish. They would try anyway. The boss probably thought they were already dead. They would thwart his plan as long as they could.

"Do you think we have a chance?" she asked him.

She was thinking that a chance might exist. That was more than she had the day before. He again tried to be reassuring. "Our situation is certainly precarious," he said. "But it is not hopeless. We have a shelter, such as it is. We have water. There are fish in the sea, and we have a way to catch them. I think we will eventually catch a fish. There is just one problem I am concerned about." As soon as he said it, he wished he had not. He needed to stop thinking out loud.

"What is the problem?" she asked.

It was inevitable that she would ask. He figured he might as well tell her. "Seals eat fish," he answered.

"Why is that a problem?" she wanted to know. "Aren't there enough for them and us?"

"Yes, there are," he said. "That's not the problem."

She persisted, "Well then, what's the problem?"

He didn't want to answer, but he knew he had to, "Polar bears eat seals."

Chapter 5 I Won't Eat You

They settled down to their second night in their new home. At least, it was not any colder than the first night. They knew it soon would be colder, much colder. In the morning they went to their "water fountain" and got another drink. Then they went right to the task of trying to catch a fish. They saw fish, but they couldn't catch any. Either the fish were too far away to reach them with their net, or they were too quick to catch. It was very frustrating, and they were getting more and more hungry. They tried all day, but they just couldn't catch any fish. Finally, as it was getting dark, they returned to the rough enclosure they called home. Needless to say, they were very discouraged.

"Do you think we will starve?" she asked.

He wanted to encourage her, but he didn't want to give false hope. "I just don't know," he replied. "We certainly are not doing very well at fishing, and that seems to be our only hope for food at this point."

They were both silent for a time. Then she said, "You are always talking about the Eskimos. Did many of them starve?"

He was uneasy contemplating how he should respond. He knew many of the Eskimos did starve in the old days. Should he tell her that? As a journalist, he was in the habit of telling the truth even when he knew some people would not like it. He always insisted people had a right to know the truth. He finally decided he would be honest with her. It really couldn't make things any worse. "Starvation was one of the greatest challenges the Eskimos faced. That was one of the reasons they moved around a lot. When game became scarce in one area, they would move on to another area where hunting looked more promising. It is interesting that one of their main deities was one they called 'The Old Woman Who Sent Out the Game.' Finding food consumed most of their time."

"You are not being very helpful," she responded. "What happened if they couldn't find food?"

The answer was quite obvious. "They died."

She didn't like his answer. "But didn't they try to do something to stay alive?" She just didn't want to accept reality.

"Of course," he replied. "Sometimes they would even eat bird droppings. Some resorted to cannibalism. Normally, they were not cannibals, but when people are desperate, they do things they would not do otherwise. Sometimes mothers would kill their children to save them from a slow death from starvation."

"That's horrible!" she said in disgust.

"I agree, but from their perspective, it was an act of mercy. Would you really want to watch your children slowly die of starvation?"

"I suppose not. But it just seems like there would have to be another way."

He thought of the stories he had read. Then he remembered one that had a happy ending. "I remember reading about one Eskimo man who survived a time of starvation. He overheard a couple of women saying they were going to kill his sister to keep from starving. He told her about their plan, and they decided to run away. Fortunately, they did manage to find food, and they lived for many years. In fact, he ended up marrying his sister. He said it worked out well. He not only was able to save his sister's life, but he also got a good wife as a result."

"He married his sister?"

"That's right. In their society there were no rules against incest."

"Wait a minute. Did I understand correctly that those women were going to eat the girl?"

"That's right. They were desperate. Actually, among the Eskimos, women were more inclined to resort to cannibalism than men. It was common to find two men who had starved together, but there were seldom two women who starved together. Usually, one would eat the other before she died herself.

She was sickened by what he was telling her, but she didn't doubt what he said. They sat quietly for a few minutes thinking about their plight. Then she said soberly, "Don't worry. I won't eat you."

"Nor I you. Life is precious, but there are limits to what we should do to survive. I would prefer death to cannibalism."

They were both silent again. Then he said, "Let's not focus on death. Let's concentrate on how we can stay alive. We need to catch a fish. It is dark now. In the morning we will try again. For now the best we can do is to try to get some rest."

With that they settled down to another cold night in the far north.

Chapter 6 What is an Eskimo?

They awoke in the morning cold, hungry and thirsty. At least, they knew what to do about their thirst. After getting a drink, they went about their quest for a fish with renewed determination. They knew that if they didn't succeed, their determination not to eat each other would be sorely tested. It was not that they lacked resolve, but it was becoming increasingly clear that catching a fish was a matter of life or death. After trying for an hour or so, they decided to look around the island for a better location. They spent some time looking only to conclude that their original choice was the best. They tried for another hour. By that time she was so cold that they both agreed that she should return to the shelter.

He continued his seemingly hopeless task. Why couldn't he catch a fish? He could see them in the water, but they were usually too far away. Once or twice one did get within range, but it always managed to escape. How could he attract them so that he would have a better chance of getting the net under one? What attracts fish? He tried to think. He needed something for bait. Then he remembered that a big nuisance in the Arctic in the summer is insects. Often the caribou will find a patch of ice or snow to rest on because the insects don't like the cooler air over those places. Summer was over, but maybe he could find some dead insects. He set his net aside for a while and looked around. Sure enough he did manage to find what he was looking for.

He returned to the shore and threw a couple bugs on the water. The fish didn't seem to notice them. How could he get their attention? He remembered reading somewhere that sharks can smell blood in the water from a long distance away. Most fish have a good sense of smell. Maybe he could try scratching his arm to get some blood. He tried it and then put a drop of blood on an insect and threw it in the water. After a minute or so a cod about ten inches long came up to the surface and swallowed the bug. Then it swam away. Why didn't he have his net ready? He tried again. This time he had to wait for five minutes before a fish accepted his invitation. He almost caught it, but it slipped just over his net and escaped.

He still had not caught anything, but he was learning. He noticed the direction the fish usually went in trying to escape. If he could get his net between the fish and its escape route, maybe he could succeed. He tried again. It almost worked, but the fish was too small and managed to slip through the holes in the net. After several more tries, a fish that looked like the one who took his first bait came up for a meal. He pulled up on the net. The fish sensed danger and retreated, but it ran into the net. He quickly yanked it up on the shore and jumped on it. He wanted to make sure the fish didn't jump back into the water. It

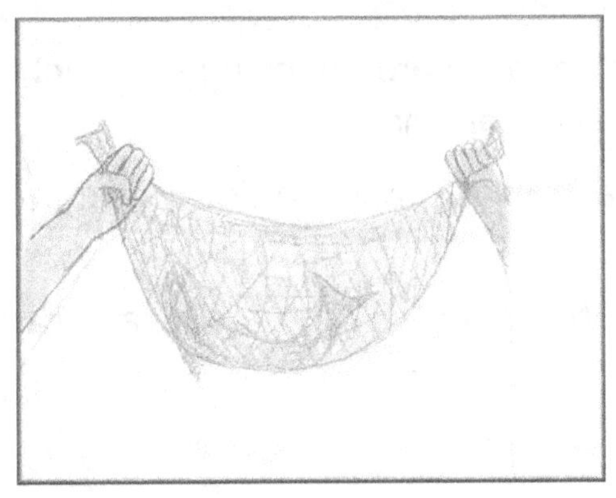
Figure 2 The Hair Net

thrashed around for a while, but he didn't dare get off it for fear it might escape. For the first time they had food, and he couldn't take a chance of losing it. After the fish was still for some time, he slowly rolled off it, making sure he rolled toward the water so that if it started flopping around again, it was less likely to get back to the sea. The net was still around the fish. He grabbed the net and fish with both hands and headed inland. He didn't want to take any chance of losing this food they had tried so hard to obtain.

He stopped and looked at the fish. Then it sunk in what had just happened. He had obtained food. They would not starve. At least, if they did, it would not be soon. Suddenly, he was excited. He had to hurry back to the shelter to share the good news with her.

As soon as he entered the stone igloo, he showed her his catch and said, "Look. I got a fish. Isn't that great?"

At first, she looked on in stunned silence. Then she began to smile. "You caught a fish. You actually caught a fish. Let me see it." She grabbed the fish and gave it a hug. She couldn't have been more excited if she had just been given the crown jewels. She knew this meant life instead of death. After a minute of jubilation, she decided it was time to be practical. "Okay, this is great. How do we cook it?"

"We don't"

"What do you mean? We certainly are not going to mount it and put it over the fireplace we don't have."

"Exactly. We don't have a fireplace, and we don't have any way to make a fire."

"Then what can we do? We certainly can't eat it raw, can we?"

"Yes"

"You can't be serious. Surely the Eskimos didn't eat their meat raw."

"Do you know what the word 'Eskimo' means?"

"No. What difference does that make?"

"It is commonly believed that it means 'eater of raw meat'. Some dispute that definition. They claim it means 'he laces snowshoes'. That is questionable since all the native people of northern Alaska and Canada used snowshoes. There are other meanings suggested as well, such as, 'people of a different land', 'people of dark skin', and 'people of different behavior'. Whether 'eater of raw meat' is the original meaning of the word or not, they did and still do eat some of their meat raw.”

“Yuck! Why would they call themselves something so gross?”

“It was probably their enemies that called them that. In Canada today “Eskimo” is considered to be a derogatory term, but in Alaska and many other places it is still considered acceptable.”

“What word is used in Canada?”

“'Inuit' is the most common term. It is what they call themselves. Actually, the word refers to the native people of northern Canada and Greenland. The Eskimos of Siberia and Alaska are Yupik. There are several subgroups. Then there are the Aleuts.”

“Aren't they the ones the Aleutian Islands are named for?”

“That's right. Many of them are part Russian because Russia controlled that part of North America until the United States bought Alaska in 1867.”

“Yes, but do we really have to eat the fish raw? Won't it make us sick?”

“It didn't make the Eskimos sick. Seals don't cook the fish they eat either.”

“They're animals.”

“That's true, but Eskimos are people. Look, I would rather cook the fish too, but we just don't have that option.”

“Well, okay, but I don't like the idea.”

With that they proceeded to eat the fish. He insisted on keeping the entrails to use for bait. Arctic cod eat a wide variety of things. One thing mature cod eat is younger cod. He thought that meant they could be attracted by the fish remains.

They had managed to obtain food. If they could continue to catch fish, maybe they would not starve. There was still a serious question about whether or not they could keep from freezing. It would get much colder before the winter was over. If they could survive the winter, maybe they could eventually find a way off the island and back to civilization. He began to formulate a plan of action.

Chapter 7 Where Are We?

He knew that if they were to return to civilization, they first needed to have some idea where they were. They had been flying mostly north, but it was not straight north. If it had been, they would have flown over part of Hudson Bay. He knew they had not flown far enough east to have missed the entire bay. Therefore they must have gone far enough west to miss it. That gave them a rough idea of their longitude. What was their latitude?

She could tell he was deep in thought about something. "How about if you let me in on whatever you are plotting?"

"I am trying to figure out where we are so that we can formulate a strategy to get back home."

"I thought you said you figured we were between Ellesmere Island and Victoria Island."

"That is my guess. The bigger question is how far north we are."

"Is there any way to know?"

"Actually, latitude should be easier to determine than longitude. The only way to know the longitude is to have a clock set at Greenwich Mean Time and then determine the exact local time of noon. We can't do that. We can get a close estimate of latitude though."

"How do we do that?"

"There are a couple of ways. We could make a protractor and quadrant. If it were not past the autumnal equinox, we could measure the angle of the sun at noon. Since it is too late for that, we would need to wait for the vernal equinox. That means we need to make a calendar to keep track of the time. We can also check the angle of the North Star. We can also count the number of days of no daylight."

"I don't understand. How will that help?"

"At the North Pole there are six months of no day and six months of no night. At the Arctic Circle there is one day of no night and one day of no light. If we can count the days when the sun doesn't rise, we will have an idea how far we are from the North Pole and from the Arctic Circle."

"I think I have an idea what you are talking about, but where is the Arctic Circle?"

"It is at about sixty-six and a half degrees north latitude."

"How does that help us?"

"Well, the circumference of the earth is about 25,000 miles. That means it is a little over 6,000 miles from the equator to the North Pole. Since that is 90 degrees of latitude, just do the math. Each degree of latitude is 69 miles. If we can determine our latitude, we know how far we are from the Arctic Circle."

"Okay, but why do we want to know how far we are from the Arctic Circle?"

"The Arctic Circle runs through the Arctic mainland. If we head toward the Arctic Circle, we will reach the mainland first."

"I see. If we know our latitude, we know how far we are from the Arctic Circle."

"That's right."

"So, how far do you think it is?"

"I can only guess until we can get a measurement, but I think we are somewhere near Resolute on Cornwallis Island. If that is true, we are about 500 miles from the mainland."

"Why don't we just go to Resolute?"

"We don't know which direction it is. We would just be wandering about aimlessly. It would really be nice if we could find it because it has nearly 200 people and an airport that can serve fairly large jet planes."

"Stop it. Just stop it."

"Stop what?"

"Stop lying to me."

"I'm not lying. Resolute really does have a large airport. Its runway is nearly two miles long. You can fly from there to Yellowknife, Edmonton, Winnipeg and several other cities."

"That's not what I mean."

"What is it then?"

"Stop trying to make me think we have a chance of survival. You are going to get my hopes up only to disappoint me. You caught one little fish, and now you think all our problems are over. We are still going to freeze, and even if we don't, you said yourself there is no way off the island because we don't have a boat."

"We don't have to have a boat."

"Why not? Do you think we can just walk off the island?"

"Yes."

"Oh, great! Now you think you can walk on water. You must think you are somebody really special."

"Anybody can walk on water. You just have to wait for it to freeze."

"But you said yourself that saltwater doesn't freeze."

"I didn't say it doesn't freeze. I said it doesn't freeze until it gets to about twenty-eight degrees."

"How cold does it get here?"

"About forty below zero. It has gotten down to ninety below. In Antarctica the temperature has fallen to 129 below."

"I suppose next you are going to tell me how lucky we are to be in the Arctic instead of the Antarctic."

"That's true. Not only is it warmer here, but there is also more to eat."

"Stop it. I don't want to hear about any more of our big 'advantages'. When is it going to freeze so that we can walk off this godforsaken pile of rocks?"

"Sometime in October. That is when temperatures average in the teens. But we can't leave yet. We need to prepare."

"When can we leave?"

"If we survive the winter, maybe we can try to leave next winter. We need food, better clothes, weapons and a sled."

She was silent. There seemed to be little chance of survival, and if they did survive, they had to face over a year of cold, hunger and danger. What was the point of trying?

He realized he had discouraged her, but what he had said was true. They really did not have a chance of leaving the island until the next winter. The big problem would be to survive the winter that was about to begin. It was questionable if they could catch enough fish to keep from starving, and they certainly could not keep from freezing with the clothes and shelter they had. Then there was the danger from polar bears. There were none on the island, but he knew bears often swim thirty miles. On some occasions they swim much farther. He tried to engage her in conversation, but she was so despondent that she didn't want to talk.

He decided to proceed with his plan to determine their location. The simplest way to get an immediate estimate of the latitude was to find the angle from the horizon to the North Star. There was not much to work with, but he found a large flat rock. He was able to persuade her to donate a few more of her long blond hairs. He attached a pebble to the hair to act as a plumb line. When it was dark, he was able to get her to go outside with him to help hold the rock and the plumb line while he sighted the North Star. As nearly as he could determine the angle from the sight line to the plumb line was about fifteen degrees. That meant they were at about seventy-five degrees north latitude, which was about the latitude of Resolute. If only they knew if it was east or west of them, but they had no way of knowing. Since there is regular air travel to and from Resolute, maybe they could see a plane. They would watch and hope.

Chapter 8 The Stick

Over the next few days they continued to try to catch fish with the crude net they had made. Some days they were successful, but more often than not they weren't. On some occasions he was sure he could have gotten a fish if he just had a spear. He could fashion a spear head from the stones, but he really needed something to attach it to. Driftwood sometimes makes it to the Arctic islands, but there is little as far north as they were.

One day as they were fishing, he noticed something in the water a couple hundred feet from the shore. It drifted toward them. As it got closer, he could see that it was a stick of wood. That was just what he needed to make his spear. Would it come to shore?

"Look," he said. "There is a piece of wood floating in the water."

"What good does that do us? You said we can't burn wood. We can't even start a fire."

He watched in consternation as the stick floated along. It was going to miss the island.

"We have to get that stick," he said earnestly.

"Are you crazy? There is no way to get to it."

"I will try to swim to it."

"You really are crazy. It's freezing. You wouldn't last one minute out there."

"A strong man can usually survive five minutes in freezing water."

"You're not that strong. Don't try it!"

"I have to."

"No, don't!"

Figure 3 The Stick

The stick was going to get away. He jumped into the freezing water and swam out to it. By then he was becoming numb. He grabbed the stick and headed back to shore. She looked on in horror as he slowed to a stop only halfway back.

"Come on. Keep going," she yelled.

"I can't," he responded. His limbs simply would not move anymore because of the cold. The situation was desperate.

As she watched from the shore, she knew he was about to die. If he died, she would die. Not only so, but she would die all alone. What could she do? Without thinking, she rushed out into the water. It was only half as far as he had gone to reach stick. When she got to him, she grabbed him and headed back toward shore. It was slower progress dragging his inert body. The cold was rapidly taking over. Would she be able to get back to shore before she too became too numb to continue? She knew the lives of both of them depended on her ability to get to land. Swimming was slow, and she was getting slower because her arms and legs just didn't want to move. Then her feet touched ground. She renewed her efforts. It was difficult, but she managed to get him to dry ground.

He was still holding the stick. She was angry. He had risked his life for a worthless piece of wood. She grabbed it and threw it into the water. Then it occurred to her that if he had wanted it that badly, maybe she should keep it. She waded the short distance to it and threw it back on land. Then she approached him. He was motionless.

"Well, there's your stick you wanted so bad. I hope you are satisfied. I told you not to try it. You always think you are so smart. Why couldn't you listen to me for once?" She didn't know if he was alive or not. Being angry was the only way she could think of to deal with the situation. She continued, "I hate you. It's all your fault we got stuck here, and now I will have to die all alone because you were so dumb you got yourself killed for nothing. I hate you! I hate you!" With that she slapped his face.

He was still conscious, but he couldn't move. He knew he would die if he passed out. Without knowing it, she had done just what was needed. The slap helped him stay awake. How could he communicate with her when he couldn't move?

She was fighting hysteria and hypothermia at the same time. She tried to think rationally. He had said earlier that one man had been revived after his body temperature had dropped to 56.7 degrees. Was he still alive, and if so, could he be revived? She tried her best to keep her wits about her. How could she tell if he was still alive? She checked to see if he was breathing. He didn't seem to be. What about a heartbeat? She couldn't tell. Then she thought about checking his eyes. She pulled up his eyelids. That was what he needed. He couldn't move, but he was able to focus his eyes on her. As she looked into his eyes, she could tell there was some sign of life there. She was excited, but she couldn't bring herself to show it. "I told you before not to stare at me."

She closed his eyelids again. He was alive. That was great. They had a chance. She tried to think of what to do. If he could be warmed up, he might live. How could she warm him up when there was no heat on the island? The only place that was even a little warmer was in their shelter. That was all she could think of.

She tried to pick him up, but it was no use. She was numb from the cold herself, and he outweighed her by nearly fifty pounds. She tried dragging him, but that was too hard. Next she tried to crawl under him, but that didn't work. Finally, she lay down on her back on top of him and tried to roll over holding his arm. It took a few tries, but it worked. Now she was under him. She struggled to get to her hands and knees. When she did, she tried walking that way. It was difficult, and it hurt her knees. She tried to get to her feet, but he was heavy. Under normal circumstances she might have made it, but the combination of cold, fatigue and lack of food made her too weak. Then she had an idea. The rocks were uneven. If she could walk on her hands and knees to a spot where they were at different levels, she could step down and straighten her legs. It worked. Now she was on her hands and legs. It was an awkward position. She needed to straighten up more, but he was too heavy. Then she thought that if it worked for her legs, it should work for her upper body. She found another spot where the rocks were uneven and managed to get to a more upright position. Then she shifted the weight so that it was centered over her legs. Now she could walk.

He was heavy, and she was weak. It took all her strength to carry him. The best she could do was to walk a few steps and then rest. The rest was not much help. She still had the weight of his body to carry, and she didn't dare to set him down because she knew she couldn't pick him up again. Normally it would have been a five-minute walk to the shelter, but because of the difficulty of carrying him, it took nearly half an hour. Actually, that was good because the extreme effort caused her body to warm. Her body heat in turn helped warm him.

When she reached the shelter, she dropped to the ground. It had taken all the strength she could muster to get that far. She lay there gasping for breath for a few minutes. As soon as she could, she dragged his limp body inside and blocked off the entrance. They had replaced one of the stones on the top of the enclosure with a piece of ice to let in a little light. That was good because otherwise it would have been completely dark.

Now she had succeeded in getting him into the room. How could she warm him up? Their crude home was the warmest place on the island, but it was still so cold she could see her breath. She was still breathing hard as she tried to think of a solution. Then it hit her. She was looking right at it. Her breath was the warmest thing on the island. It wouldn't be enough to warm his whole body, but she could warm his face.

She cupped her hands around his face and blew her warm breath onto it. Then she remembered that the owner of the restaurant had required all his employees to learn CPR in case someday one of the customers needed it. She could blow warm air into his lungs. For several minutes she alternated between CPR and blowing warm air onto his face. Would it work?

He was still fighting to stay conscious. What she was doing was helping, but he wanted desperately to communicate with her. She was blowing air into his lungs. His vocal cords were deep enough inside his body to still function, but he couldn't move his tongue or lips. If he could make the air pass over his vocal cords, maybe he could get enough sound to let her know he was still conscious. He tried. All he could produce was "Hhhhhh."

She heard the sound and recognized he was trying to say something. He was alive. Even if he could never use his arms and legs again, at least he might be able to talk. That was something. She was thrilled, but she felt that she had to keep up the tough exterior. "Are you trying to say something? Well, speak up. I can't understand you." Of course, she knew he couldn't talk. If he really was trying to communicate, maybe it would help if she could loosen his mouth. She had been warming his face with her breath. If she could move his mouth, maybe he could regain enough control to speak. "If you're too lazy to move your lips, let me help you. I don't know why I always have to do everything for you." She was just babbling because she felt like she had to say something.

He tried to speak again. "Hhhhhhiii." His tongue was able to move a little, but his lips were still too numb.

She could tell they were making progress. "Well, come on. Try a little harder."

He was trying as hard as he could. "Hhhhiiiiiit." He managed to move his tongue enough to make a "t" sound.

She responded, "It sounded like you said 'hit'. What are you trying to say?"

He tried again, "Hhiit."

"Do you want me to hit you? You really are crazy." She thought about it. Maybe that was what he was trying to say. A slap might help stimulate him. She had slapped him before in anger. Now she felt guilty, but she couldn't bring herself to admit it. "You certainly have a good slap coming after doing such a stupid thing. You could have gotten yourself killed. It really is true that men are just little boys grown tall. They still need a mommy to take care of them. Here, take that." She hit him on the cheek, being careful not to hit too hard. Would it help? She looked for some sign of a response. There was nothing. She slapped him on each cheek a few more times. Then she grabbed his head and shook it. "Come on, you. Do something. Don't just sit there like a bump on a log." She slapped his cheek again, but this time she hit harder.

His face began to shiver uncontrollably. That was good. The body was trying to fight for recovery. He tried to speak again with his quivering mouth. "Aggggain."

"You want me to hit you again?" she asked excitedly. He was finally responding. "Well, okay, you asked for it." She slapped his face back and forth a few more times.

"Enough," he finally said. He was feeling the pain now. That was a sign the blood was circulating in his face again. His whole face was shaking. The white color was being replaced by pink. It hurt, but he was glad. He knew that meant he was recovering from the cold.

The next question was whether or not he could regain the use of his limbs. There was no feeling in his arms or legs. He knew that the longer they went without proper blood circulation, the poorer would be his chances of restoring proper function. He instructed her to move his arms back and forth. At first there was no reaction. Then he began to feel pain. Pain was feeling. If there was no feeling, that would mean his arms were dead. He asked her to stop. The pain was getting worse. He moaned, but there was no escape. She felt sorry for him, but there was nothing she could do. He tried to move his arms to find a less painful position. At first, he couldn't move them, but eventually he succeeded. To begin with he could only move the arms. Then he was able to bend the elbows. It would take time before the hands would be restored. He thought it would be wise to get blood flowing to his legs. She moved them back and forth until he could move them himself. It took some time, and it was painful, but little by little all his extremities returned to normal.

After such an ordeal they were both exhausted. They needed rest. He thought it wise if one of them stayed awake while the other slept. She rested first. Then he woke her and took his turn sleeping. She fully intended to stay awake, but after an hour or so she dozed off. In the morning she awoke first. She was embarrassed that she had failed to remain alert. What if he had stopped breathing or something else had gone wrong? Fortunately, nothing had. She decided it was time to wake him up. When he became fully alert, he noticed that it was light again.

"You didn't have to stay awake all night." he said.

She was tempted to pretend that she had stayed awake, but that would not be honest. Since they were stuck with each other, it would be important that they be able to trust each other. "Actually, I'm afraid I fell asleep."

"I see. Well, I guess no harm was done."

They were silent for a while. Then he said, "You saved my life."

She wasn't sure how to respond. "Well, it was your own fault. If you hadn't tried to get that stick, there would not have been any problem." That didn't seem like the right thing to say.

He replied, "I just wanted to thank you."

"You're welcome," was her only response. Surely she should say something else. She was really relieved that he had survived. How could she tell him that without letting down her defenses? Finally she decided to just say it. "I'm glad you are still alive."

He noticed that it was getting darker in the shelter. "How long did I sleep?" he asked.

"Just over night."

"Then why is it getting dark already?"

"I don't know. Maybe something is blocking the light."

He opened the entrance and found that there was an inch of snow covering everything.

"Where is the stick?"

"I left it on the shore."

"It will be covered with snow. I'll go get it."

With that he ran to the place where they had been the day before and retrieved the stick. After returning to their home he examined it. Someone had fashioned it into a tool or weapon before. It had probably been a spear. The head was missing, and it appeared that it had broken off. Someone had had an unsuccessful hunt. It had been a spear before, and it would be a spear again.

Chapter 9 Prepare and Beware

"Oh no," she said. "Everything is covered with snow."

"Actually, that is good."

"Are you going to tell me the snow is another advantage? I suppose if the whole earth were crashing into the sun, you would think that was somehow a good thing."

"It would certainly warm things up for us, wouldn't it?"

"Stop it. You're not funny. Why is the snow a good thing?"

"There are several reasons. For one thing it brightens things up. It was getting a little dreary. More importantly, snow is great insulation. We can shovel it over our igloo to increase protection from the cold. Also, snow is fresh water. Our supply was getting a little low. Later on, when we leave the island, we can use the snow to make an igloo to stay in temporarily. Another nice thing about snow is that it makes it easier to pull a sled. You see, there are many good uses for snow."

"All I know is that snow is cold, and I don't like cold."

"It may be cold, but it will help keep us warm. Let's see if we can shovel some onto our snug little nest."

It took some time, but they were able to add a layer of snow to the rocks that they called home. It would help some. Then they returned to the interior of their snow-covered stone shelter. They were both still weary from the trauma of the previous day. He had already selected a stone that he thought would work for a spearhead. He began chipping away at it to give it the desired shape. She just watched silently as he worked. Would the spear really help? She hoped so, but it was obvious that they would need more than just a spear to survive. He had said it would get to forty below zero during the winter. It was already so cold she could hardly stand it. As she watched, a thought occurred to her.

"How do you plan to attach the spearhead to the stick?"

"We need something long and flexible that is strong enough to hold them together."

"I know where this is going. You want more of my hair, don't you?"

"That's a good idea. Thanks for volunteering. "

"I didn't say I was volunteering. First, you want my hair for your net. Then you want more for your plumb line. Now you want it for your stupid spear. Before we are done I will be completely bald."

"It will grow back."

"I know. Oh, okay. I suppose we have no choice. I don't know how I let you talk me into these things."

"I do. You want to stay alive just as I do. The Eskimos survived because they learned to use everything they had at their disposal. We must do the same. It is fortunate you have such nice long hair."

"At least there is something about me that you think is nice."

"You saved my life yesterday. That was nice."

"That is something I did. It is not something about me."

"I'm sure you have a number of fine qualities."

That didn't seem very personal. Then she realized that she was being a little too forward. Maybe he would think she was fishing for compliments. They had been through a lot already, and they would probably be together for some time, but she really didn't know him very well. If only she had not overheard that conversation, they would not have been thrown together like this. Of all the eating places in Chicago, why did the syndicate choose the one where she worked? There was not much point to dwelling on that now. She returned to the matter at hand.

"Okay, how much hair do you want this time?" She knew that didn't sound very nice. It was as much for her survival as it was his. Why couldn't she bring herself to at least be a little cordial? She told herself it was because he was rather cool toward her, but she knew that was not it. Maybe it was just the stress of their situation. She had always managed to be pleasant with the customers. Why couldn't she act the same now? Of course, they were paying money. He had just kept her alive. Okay, that was something.

By the end of the day he was satisfied with his spearhead. He proceeded to place it on the stick and wrap it with hair. She thought he was using more hair than necessary, but he explained that they wanted to be sure that it was secure.

"If we have to use it for protection from polar bears, it needs to be strong."

"You keep talking about polar bears. We have been all over the island. There are no bears here."

"Not yet, but they may come."

"We are surrounded by water as far as the eye can see. Just how far do you think a bear can swim?"

"One bear swam 426 miles in the Beaufort Sea. It took her nine days, and she lost 22 percent of her body weight. That is the record as of now."

"426 miles! Are you sure? That's a long way."

"Bears have amazing endurance. I heard of one that ran a whole mile after being shot in the heart. Of course, the younger ones are not as strong. The cub of the record setting bear died along the way."

"Oh, the poor thing. That is so sad."

"Polar bears are very dangerous animals. If that cub had grown up and if he were here now, he would kill you. We must beware."

She knew he was right, but she still thought of a cub as a nice soft teddy bear. Why did the real world have to be so cruel?

The spear was finished. At least they had some protection, and maybe they could catch a few more fish. He knew the sea would soon freeze over for the winter. That would make fishing more difficult. Where there are fish, there may be seals. They had not seen any yet, but when the ocean was frozen enough, they could walk over the ice in search of breathing holes. Seals are air-breathing mammals. No matter how cold it gets, they have to keep the holes open. They can stay under water for fifteen to twenty minutes. In fact, elephant seals can hold their breath for two hours. But sooner or later a seal has to have air. The Eskimos knew that, and they would often stand motionless over a breathing hole for hours waiting for a seal to come up for air. Then one quick, well-placed blow on the head would knock the seal unconscious, and he would be pulled up onto the ice. Then there would be meat to eat, seal oil for the lamps and skin for mukluks and tents.

She kept thinking about what he had said about polar bears. It was obvious that they were one of his main worries. Even though she didn't want to think about it, her curiosity finally got the best of her. "Do you really think bears are a big problem?"

"Yes"

"How big?"

"A female polar bear can weigh 550 pounds."

"Wow! That's big. Are the males bigger?"

"Yes"

"How much bigger? Come on. Tell me."

"Okay, you asked. A male polar bear can be ten feet tall and weigh as much as 1700 pounds."

"You're kidding. That's as big as a buffalo. How does a person survive a bear attack?"

He was hesitant to answer because he didn't want to worry her. At first he tried to fudge. "It depends on what kind of bear it is. If it is a black bear, the thing to do is to be aggressive. Make a lot of noise and throw things. If it is a brown bear, then just play dead. When the bear doesn't consider you to be a threat, it will probably leave you alone. Of course, neither plan works with polar bears. To them people are food."

"How do you survive a polar bear attack?"

"You don't."

Chapter 10 The Bear

Over the next few days they tried to catch fish. The new spear helped some, but they were only able to get enough to keep from starving. The sea was beginning to form ice crystals. It would only be a few more days before it froze over. Then it would be even harder to obtain enough to survive, and the days were getting shorter. In another month or two the sun would not rise at all. The temperatures were frequently dropping below zero at night, and they were still not even near the coldest part of the winter. Even with the progress they had made, the only real question was whether they would die from freezing or starving.

The only time of day they could stand to be outside was during the early afternoon. Even then a couple hours were all they could bear. The shelter was not much warmer, but it was the best they had. During the brief time they were out in the cold, they tried to focus all their attention on fishing. That is why they didn't notice the danger until it was too late.

He was concentrating on getting the net under a medium sized cod when he heard her scream. He looked up and saw that his worst fears had been realized. A polar bear had swum ashore on the other side of the island and was approaching them. It was between them and their igloo. There was no escape. Instinctively he grabbed the spear and stepped between her and the bear. Maybe if he could distract it, she could get around the bear and make it to the shelter. That would only delay her death a short time, but he had to do what he could.

Figure 4 The Polar Bear

He told her to try to circle around while he waved the spear in the bear's face. She got part way when the bear attacked him. He ran back a few steps and then turned to face it. It was not full grown. When it stood on its hind legs, it was about six feet tall. That is to say it was a six foot, two hundred pound killing machine that was hungry after its long swim. Would he have any chance against it with his puny spear? He didn't know, but he had no choice but to try.

He tried to keep the spear between him and the bear. If there was a chance, maybe he could get in a lucky jab. Luck was not with him. Almost faster than he could see, the bear hit him on the chest with its forepaw. He dropped to the ground motionless.

She looked on, too terrified to move. He had warned her of the danger of polar bears, and now she had seen the bear kill him with just one quick blow. She knew she would be next. What difference did it make? She knew she could not survive without him. After all their efforts to stay alive, their lives had ended abruptly with the arrival of this bear.

Suddenly, she didn't care anymore about trying to avoid death. She knew she couldn't anyway. All she could think of was that this bear had taken away what little chance of life she had. Now she was angry. There was no point in trying to escape. She knew she couldn't do anything to harm the bear, but she would at least take out her frustrations on it before she died.

The bear was standing over the man to make sure he was dead. She ran at it in a fit of rage. The bear certainly had not expected an attack from anything so small and weak. Polar bears have no enemies. They are the masters of their entire world. No one can challenge them, and yet this little creature was pounding on its back. It didn't hurt at all. The bear was more surprised than anything else. It turned around to see what was happening. She continued to beat on it. The bear finally realized it was being attacked. What presumption! No one attacks a polar bear. It rose again on its hind legs and prepared to kill this foolish attacker. It would only take one swipe of its paw.

The man was not dead. He was only stunned by the blow he had received. His chest hurt, but no ribs had been broken. He looked up to see the bear standing over her. In a moment she would be killed. He had no thought of being a hero. He was a man, and a woman was in imminent danger of death. There was only one thing to do. He grabbed his spear and rushed toward the bear. Its back was toward him. With all his strength he stabbed the spear into the bear's back.

Either by luck or by providence, the spearhead landed right in the bear's spine. It instantly dropped to the ground. He yanked out the spear and stepped back. The bear howled in pain and rage. It tried to rise to destroy the creature that had caused him the pain, but its hind legs would not respond. It tried again. It couldn't stand up. It still would not let the offense go unpunished.

Using its front legs, the bear pawed its way toward the man. He jumped back. Even a badly wounded bear can cause instant death. The bear tried again to rise, but to no effect. It lunged toward the man again. Even in its partly paralyzed condition, the bear almost caught him. This happened a couple more times. He tried to think what to do. The bear was disabled, but it was far from dead. Should he just try to stay away from the beast or try to kill it? It would not die for a long time if at all. If he tried to kill it, he might be killed.

He tried to stay out of range for a while. Then he had an idea. He had been able to stab the bear before because she had distracted it. Maybe they could use the same tactic again. He called to her to throw a rock at it. When she did, the bear turned around to see what was happening. He stepped toward it cautiously. Then the bear turned back to see him within range of its powerful front legs. This was its chance to kill the thing that had caused it so much trouble.

It gave a wrathful growl before making the kill. The man saw his chance and thrust his spear into the bear's mouth. The tip punctured the main artery going to the head. Blood poured out of its mouth. He jumped back, leaving the spear where it had landed. The bear pawed at the spear in an attempt to dislodge it. It was to no avail. The wound would prove fatal in a few minutes, as the bear's lifeblood gushed out. There was nothing to do now but wait for the loss of blood to have its effect. He stepped back to watch at a safe distance. He knew that even a badly wounded bear was still very dangerous.

He suddenly realized that he was shaking. Was it the cold, or was it the extreme danger they had just faced? Then he remembered her. Was she all right? She was standing there in a daze. She didn't seem to have been harmed physically, but it went without saying that she was greatly shaken by the experience.

"Are you okay?" he asked.

She didn't answer at first. Then she said weakly, "Yes."

He wasn't sure if she even heard him. He returned his attention to the bear. It was becoming weaker by the minute. Taking a chance, he approached. It might spring back to life at any time. Grabbing the spear, he gave it a quick pull. If the bear had had hands, it might have been able to dislodge the spear. That probably would have only accelerated the loss of blood. Anyway, he was able to retrieve his spear. He stood there for a few more minutes with the spear in hand just in case. When the bear seemed to be still, he came closer and prodded it to see if there was any life yet. When he was satisfied that it was really dead, he relaxed.

He was still shaking. They had nearly been killed. She slowly approached. When she looked at the bear, she saw all the blood. It disgusted her.

"You killed the poor animal. That's awful."

He couldn't believe his ears. That "poor animal" had nearly killed both of them, and now all she cared about was the fact that he had killed it. Maybe she would have preferred to be killed herself. All the time they had been there she had done nothing but complain. She would have been dead a long time already if it were not for him, and now she was condemning him for killing a bear that almost killed them. How could she be so stupid? How about a little appreciation for saving her life! He had tried to be patient with her, and this was the response he got. He was fed up with it, and he didn't want to take any more.

"Look, you dumb blond, don't you understand what this means?"

"Don't call me that."

"Okay, I'm sorry. It just slipped out."

"Well, if it slipped out, you must have been thinking it."

"Hey, I said I'm sorry."

"You men are all alike. You think just because a girl has blond hair she can't have any brains. What about men with blond hair? Do they have brains? You think you are so superior. I'm just as smart as you. You are nothing but an egotistical, male chauvinist pig, and I hate…" She stopped in the middle of her tirade. "Wait a minute. What did you just say?"

"I said I'm sorry I called you a dumb blond."

"No, I mean the other."

"What?"

"You said, 'don't you understand what this means?' What are you talking about?"

How could she be so dense? He was tempted to ask, but he didn't want another tongue-lashing. Apparently he would have to spell it out for her. Trying to control himself, he said, "Look at the bear."

"I don't want to."

"Come on. Look."

Reluctantly, she complied.

"What do you see?"

"A pitiful animal you killed and a lot of blood. I hate blood."

Maybe he should have let the bear kill her. But, no. That would not be right, and he really didn't want her dead. Biting his tongue, he said, "What you ought to be seeing is a hundred pounds of meat, a warm fur coat and bones to use for tools, weapons and a sled."

Slowly it began to sink in. The bear would enable them to survive the winter. Still in a bit of a daze, she said softly to herself, "I really am a dumb blond." When she realized what she had just said, she tried to back-paddle. "What I mean is…that is…well, yes. I see what you mean. A hundred pounds of meat. Yes, that would make about four hundred quarter-pounders. There are two of us. That means two hundred each. Yes, that should be enough to get us through the winter. The fur coat will keep us from freezing. The bones should help. Yes, I see. You are quite right. My thought exactly." She realized she was only making herself look more foolish. She concluded, "Okay, I'll shut up now."

He looked at her, and she looked at him. Then he began to smile. She smiled too. Then he laughed. Then she laughed. They both realized their argument was really just a result of the extreme stress they had been under.

He said, "I'll try to remember not to call you a dumb blond again."

"And I really don't think you are a male chauvinist pig, just a male chauvinist." They both laughed again.

So it was that the bear who could have been the cause of their death became the means of their life.

Chapter 11 The Winter

After a few minutes of savoring their good fortune, they decided that it was time to get practical. They had the means to survive the winter, but there was work to be done. How should they proceed? He looked at the bear and tried to formulate a plan. It was obvious that it needed to be gutted, skinned and stored in an appropriate place.

"I guess the only thing we have to use for a knife is our spearhead. Let's see what we can do."

"What should I do?" she asked.

"Well, among the Eskimos it was the job of the men to hunt the game and bring it home. The women were supposed to gut it out, skin it, share some of the meat with the neighbors and chew the hides."

"Chew the hides? Why?"

"That was to soften them and make them more usable. In fact, the Eskimo women chewed so many hides that when they got old, their teeth were worn down to the nubs."

"Look, Buster, if you think I am going to chew animal hides for you, you have another thing coming."

"Okay, I understand. Let me see if I can gut the bear."

"Oh, yuck!"

"It may be yucky, but it is a way to stay alive."

"I wish we had a way to cook it."

"So do I, but we don't."

"A hundred pounds of bear meat, and we have to eat it all raw."

"We can't eat all of it. The heart is okay, but we can't eat the liver."

"Why not?"

"It is poisonous. So is wolf and dog liver. On the other hand, the Eskimos considered seal liver to be a great delicacy, but it depends on the type of seal."

"What would happen if we ate the liver?"

"There are some lesser problems like sluggishness, headache and irritability, but one of the biggest problems is severe skin peeling. It can even result in death."

"What cases the problem?"

"Excessive levels of Vitamin A."

"I thought Vitamin A was something we need."

"It is, but high levels become toxic."

"Are there other animals in the Arctic that have poisonous livers?"

"Yes. The walrus and moose both must be avoided too."

With that they set to work. It took some time because the spearhead was not as sharp as a regular knife, but they managed to cut the bear open and remove the intestines. She wanted to throw them into the ocean, but he insisted on keeping everything because he knew that they would need every bit for their survival.

"What possible use could we have for intestines?" she asked.

"Actually, they are quite important. They can be used for rope and string for tying things and sewing. The Eskimo women became quite expert at sewing. They could make a seam that was completely waterproof. An Eskimo could tip over in his kayak and get nothing wet but his face."

"But I don't see what good it does us to have string when we don't have any needles to sew with."

"The Eskimos used many things for needles. One of their favorites was walrus tusk. They also used bones from birds and other animals. We have polar bear bones. I think we can use them."

"I did do some sewing when I was growing up. Maybe I can give it a try." She was glad there was a skill she had that he did not. It made her feel more useful.

It took an hour to process the bear. Normally it would have been much less, but it was cold, and the spear was not the most effective knife. They needed to get the carcass to their shelter. Both of them took hold of the skin and pulled. It was difficult, but they managed to get it to the opening of the stone igloo. There they had to stop. It was too big to draw inside all at once. Taking one piece of meat at a time, they got all of it inside. There was no need to be concerned about spoilage since it was freezing in their home. Then they brought in the hide. This was the thing they really needed most at the moment. They were both shivering from the cold. Even though the hide was still wet, they put it around themselves to warm up. A fur coat that could keep a bear from freezing while swimming in icing cold water could certainly keep people from freezing as well.

After they warmed up a bit, they decided it was time for their first meal of bear meat. It would have been better if they had a way to cook it, but by now they had become resigned to the fact that they would have to eat all of it raw. At least they had enough meat for a more normal meal. Naturally, she was curious to know what the Eskimos did when they had a large amount of meat.

"Did the Eskimos gorge themselves when they killed a large animal, or did they ration the meat to make it last?"

"Actually, they normally did eat a lot when they made a major kill. Then when food was scarce, they endured stoically. Since life was so precarious, they didn't make a lot of plans for the future. I know that seems strange since they were so expert at survival."

"Well, I want to survive. Now we have the means. It seems to me that we should ration the meat. What do you think?"

For once he agreed. He was about to say that, but then he thought that it would sound like he disagreed with everything else she had said. They would be together for quite some time, and it was important that they get along. He responded, "Yes, you are right. It will be five or six months before we can reasonably expect to get any significant amount of new meat. I think we should limit ourselves to a half pound of meat per day. That will get us through to spring, and maybe we can get a few fish. If we are lucky, maybe we can even get a seal or two. Now that we have a warm fur coat, we can stand to be outside more. As soon as the ocean freezes, I will walk around the area to see if I can find seal breathing holes. We could really use seal skin. We need mukluks."

Here she interrupted, "I suppose you expect me to ask what mukluks are. I already know. They are Eskimo boots. I have seen them in catalogs. In fact, they are popular with a lot of celebrities."

"Right again, but we are not concerned about making a fashion statement. We need to keep our feet from freezing. Mukluks can be made from several kinds of skins, but seal skin is most common."

For the first time they had a real chance of making it through the winter. She had hope. They had food. They had a fur coat. Maybe they could get mukluks. They would soon be able to walk across the ice. The island had begun to feel like a prison. If they could just get beyond the shore, they would feel a little freer. Maybe they could get back to civilization.

Then she looked around the shelter. It was small and cold and dark. Back in Chicago she had complained that her apartment was too small. Now it seemed like a mansion. Then she thought of her parents' home in Vancouver. Why had she ever left? It seemed like a fun adventure to go to a big Mid-Western city. Then this nightmare had happened. She never wanted to go to Chicago again.

While she thought about the pros and cons of her past and future, he was trying to be practical. It was October. The ocean was about to freeze. The days were rapidly becoming shorter. He wanted to see what day the sun would set for the winter. That was important because it would tell them how close his estimate was of their latitude. He remembered reading about Resolute. It was at 75 degrees north latitude. That was about the same as he had calculated for their location. The sun set for the winter on November 5th at Resolute. If it set before or after November 5th, they would know that they were either north or south of the 75th parallel. He wondered why they had not seen any planes. If they were close to Cornwallis Island, they should have seen planes coming and going from the airport there. Then they could simply follow the planes. Since they had seen none, they must be a long way from the airport.

They were both immersed in their own thoughts. After a time it began to get dark. They were still cold, but the fur coat made it bearable. They had had enough to eat for a change, and they were both tired after the excitement of the day. The coat would have to suffice for a blanket. It was a little small, but if it had been bigger, the bear would have been the one sleeping in it with a full belly.

In the morning he wrapped the fur coat around himself and went outside. She urged him to hurry back because it was cold and she needed the fur to keep from freezing. When he looked around, it occurred to him that he should get rid of the blood on the snow. It might attract other polar bears. They can smell blood at least 20 miles away. They had been fortunate to kill one bear, but they probably would not be able to kill another. He proceeded to throw the blood covered snow into the water. The wind and current carried it away. At least any bear smelling it would be led somewhere else. When he returned to the igloo, she asked why he had taken so long. After hearing his explanation, she decided that shivering a little longer was worth it if it kept the other bears away.

So began the long, cold days of winter. Just a few days after the episode with the bear, the sea did freeze over. For a week or so they broke the ice to try to catch fish. They did get a couple, but it soon seemed like too much effort for what little meat they got. Each day they took turns wearing the fur coat to go outside to get exercise and fresh air. The ice got thicker and thicker every day. Finally, it was thick enough that he thought it was safe to walk on it. He began walking around the island on the ice to look for seal breathing holes. There were fish, and there had been at least one polar bear. It seemed like there should be seals.

After thoroughly searching the area for seals without success, he decided to explore in every direction to see if there were any other islands around. With over 36,000 islands in the Canadian Arctic and many of them quite large, they shouldn't be very far from another island. She didn't like the idea. "I don't want to be left here all alone in the cold. What if you don't return? How will I know what happened to you?"

"There is some risk, but I think we should try. If there is an island near us, we want to know about it. If not, we need to know that too."

"How far do you plan to go?"

"I will go a half day straight south. Then I will come back. Then I will do the same tomorrow going north. Then I will try east and west. If I find nothing, at least we will know that we are many miles from any other island."

"But what if you don't come back? What should I do?"

"It probably would not do any good to come looking for me. If I am alive, I will return. If not, you could not help me. At least you would have food to last twice as long."

"That's not much comfort."

"I know, but we need to learn what we can about our surroundings."

She fell silent. He was right of course, but she didn't relish the idea of sitting alone all day in the igloo. Even though they had piled a lot of snow over it for insulation, it was still very cold. What if he didn't return? He had the coat. She would certainly freeze without it long before the meat ran out. Even if she made it to spring, she couldn't live very long without him. She wished she could dissuade him from going, but she knew she couldn't. He hadn't listened to her when she tried to talk him out of swimming out to get the stick, and he wouldn't listen now. Then she was there to rescue him. This time she wouldn't be around if he were in danger, and even if she were, she probably couldn't help. She wanted to go with him, but there was only one coat. She was very unhappy. Then she remembered that if he had listened to her before, they would not have gotten the stick. Then there would be no spear, and they would not have been able to kill the bear. Maybe the risk he was taking was necessary.

The next morning, he left early with his spear and enough meat for one day. He promised to watch for bears and seal holes. If the weather looked bad, he would return as soon as possible. Fortunately, the weather cooperated, and by noon he decided that he should turn around. He had seen nothing but ice. He stood on his tip toes and looked as far as he could in every direction. There was nothing. He retraced his steps. By the time he was within sight of the island, he was becoming exhausted. He slowed his pace. The last couple miles seemed to take forever. When he finally reached home, she was both angry and relieved.

"What took you so long? I thought you were going to return by evening. I nearly froze to death. Give me that fur coat. I hope you found something important out there."

"I did. I learned that there is nothing but ice for a day's walk south of us."

After resting for a day, he repeated the same walk north and then east and west. There was nothing but ice for a day's walk in any direction. At least they knew more about their surroundings. There was no point in going out onto the ice again.

A few days after November 5th the sun set for the last time. Now they knew they were a little south of the 75th parallel. That meant they were about 500 miles from the mainland. They should be able to walk to it the next winter, and long before they reached it, they should find another island. All they could do now was to hunker down for the winter.

Chapter 12 Unhappy Holidays

"How will we know what time it is when there is no sun?"

"There will still be some light in the middle of the day. Because of the refraction of the sunlight, there is twilight for a while."

"How long does that last?"

"It depends."

"It depends on what?"

"It depends on what kind of twilight you are talking about."

"Twilight is twilight. How many kinds of twilight do you think there are?"

"Three."

"Okay, Smart aleck, I know you are just dying to show off how much you know. What are the three kinds of twilight and tell me why I should care."

"The three kinds are civil, nautical and astronomical. The reason you should care is because each successive one has less light. By the way, did you know that the word *Smart aleck* goes back to 1865 and the aleck part is short for Alexander?"

"You just showed that you are a smart aleck. Who else would know that, and who would care? What about the twilight? That's what I want to know. Will there be enough light so that we can see to get around?"

"There is some light in the middle of the day all winter. When the sun is between the horizon and six degrees below the horizon, there is civil twilight. There is enough light that normal activities can continue without additional light. It lasts at this latitude until the end of November. When the sun is between six and twelve degrees below the horizon, there is nautical twilight. It is still somewhat light, but extra artificial light is needed. There is nautical twilight all winter during the middle of the day. In fact, during the shortest days of the year the sun gets to within about eight degrees of the horizon. When the sun is between twelve and eighteen degrees below the horizon, there is astronomical twilight. There is a little light, but it is not enough to help much. When the sun is more than eighteen degrees below, there is no noticeable light."

"Does that mean it is completely dark?"

"No, there is still light from the moon and stars. Of course, there is also light from the aurora borealis."

"Why don't you say northern lights? I know that is what aurora borealis means. You always use big words to sound smart. That's another thing. I think you may be wrong about where we are. I saw the northern lights last night, and they seemed to be south of us. Maybe we did cross over the North Pole. That would explain why we haven't seen any planes going to Resolute."

Figure 5 Northern Lights Over the Hut

"The northern lights, as you prefer to call them, are not over the North Pole. They are normally between ten and twenty degrees south of the Pole. They are caused by the magnetic field of the earth interacting with solar radiation. Since we are about fifteen degrees south of the North Pole, sometimes the lights will be north of us and sometimes south of us."

"Are you saying we can only tell what time it is by the little bit of light we have around noon?"

"No, we can tell the time by the position of the stars. They appear to go around in a circle all day. All we have to do is to look for the location of a common constellation like the Big Dipper. The sky is like a big clock. Of course, if there are clouds, we can't see the stars. Then we don't know what time it is."

The days slowly dragged on. There was not much for them to do but to eat their frozen, raw bear meat and shiver in the cold. Naturally, they talked, but much of the time they just sat in the small, cold, dark shelter and wished spring would come. They went outside daily to get fresh air and exercise, but it was so cold, they quickly returned to huddle together under the bear skin. As each day went by, they marked it off on their calendar.

When they finally got to the fourth Thursday of November, he reminded her that it was Thanksgiving. "What a joke," she said. "What could we possibly have to be thankful for? We are freezing inside this wretched pile of rocks. We have nothing to eat but this horrible bear meat. It is so dark we can't even see each other. There is nothing to do all day but shiver in the cold, and even if we survive the winter, we don't know if we can ever get off this dreary, disgusting island. On top of all that you stink because you haven't had a bath in weeks."

"I agree completely with everything you have just said."

"You do?" she said in surprise. "I thought you would want to point out some more of our big advantages."

"Well, if you insist..."

"I didn't insist."

"Whether you did or not, we do have some things to be thankful for."

"Yeah, right. What can you think of that we can be thankful for? You remind me of the man who said, 'they told me to cheer up because things could be worse. I cheered up. Sure enough, things got worse.'"

"That's most amusing. You see? That is something to be thankful for. You still have a sense of humor."

"Oh, come on. I wasn't trying to be funny."

"I know. You were complaining. That's another thing we can be thankful for. You are still able to complain. When you can't do that anymore, then we are in big trouble."

"If it were not so dark in here, I would smack you."

"And if you were not just a girl, I would smack you."

"What do you mean *just a girl*? I'm as good as you."

It was obvious that the strain of their situation was getting to both of them. He tried to maintain his self-control. "Okay, look. We are stuck with each other whether we like it or not. Let's try to get along."

She knew he was right. They would be together for a long time, and she didn't want to act like the dumb blond he obviously thought she was. At the same time she really did want to find something about their situation that would make her feel a little less depressed. After taking a moment to regain her composure, she asked, "Okay, since you think we have it so good, what else can we be thankful for?"

"We are still alive. The boss probably thinks we have been dead for two months. While there is life, there is hope. That is one of the biggest things we can be thankful for. We have hope. If we make it through the winter, we might be able to get back home. There is enough meat to get us through the winter. It is cold, but we have a fur coat that will keep us from freezing to death. It is dark, but we have an enclosure that is better than being outside. We are shivering, but we are not sick. With no other people around, there is no one to give us their germs. Perhaps one of the best things is that we have each other."

They had each other. That was something she had not really appreciated as she should. She remembered when he almost died in the water. Then she thought about the time it looked like the bear had killed him. When he returned late from his walk across the sea, she had been so worried. How could she have such a short memory? What if he got sick and died? She would be all alone. She had just threatened to smack him. What was wrong with her? They might have their differences, but she really was glad he was there. She was thankful.

"Happy Thanksgiving," she said. "Do you think just for this special day we could have a little extra of that delicious bear meat?"

They both laughed. The bear meat was not very delectable, but it was their Thanksgiving feast.

After they had eaten she reminded him, "By the way, we are in Canada, and I am Canadian. Thanksgiving is the second Monday of October. It has been since 1957."

"Really? I didn't know that."

"Aha. I got you. I knew something you didn't."

"Hey, look, Americans and Canadians haven't fought each other since the War of 1812. Let's not start now."

"I agree. At least I got some extra meat."

The light at midday continued to be less and less. It was December now, and it was so cold they rarely went outside for more than a few minutes each day. With no sunlight the days were as cold as the nights. Neither of them had ever experienced temperatures of forty below zero. Not only did they shiver all the time, but the low temperatures made their bodies ache. How could the Eskimos stand to live in such a place?

The days dragged on ever so slowly. It was cold and dark. Inside their shelter there was no light at all. On cloudy days there was no light outside even at midday. They didn't dare eat more than their allotted amount of meat each day. If it ran out before spring, they would starve. Naturally, the strain of their existence wore on their nerves. They were both depressed, but for her sake he tried to act somewhat cheerful. It didn't work. By mid-December she was ready to give up.

"What is the point to all this? We are going to die anyway. I just can't stand any more. It is not even winter yet, and it is so cold and dreary I can't bear it."

He knew that giving up was certain death. What could he say? They had been in complete darkness for two days because of the clouds. He tried to think of something to cheer her. Then he thought of it.

"You said it is not even winter yet. That's true. Winter starts a week from today. That is the good news."

"How is that good news?"

"The first day of winter is the day of the winter solstice. That means the sun is as far south as it gets. A week from tomorrow the sun starts heading back north. Then there is Christmas, and a week later we start a new year. Just a couple weeks after that we start seeing civil twilight. By the first of February the sun will peak above the horizon again. Starting in May the sun will not set for three months. Six months from now you will be complaining that the sun is in your eyes all the time, and you can't sleep."

"That will never happen."

"Okay, prove me wrong. Live until summer."

"I know you are just trying to give me a pep talk. I would rather have a little light."

"Hang on. We'll eventually get some light."

She knew he was trying to be helpful. It would be cruel to reject his efforts. For his sake she would try to endure a little longer.

A week passed. Now it was officially winter. In a few days it would be Christmas. They both thought of their families back home. Were they mourning them because they thought they were dead? If only they could let them know they were still alive, it would be some comfort. What would it matter if they died before they could return?

Finally it was Christmas Eve. As she thought about the holidays back home, she began to cry. She missed the happy days of years past with the brightly decorated Christmas tree surrounded by presents. She missed her parents and cousins and friends. She missed the decorations and the Christmas carols and the feasts. On this particular Christmas she especially missed the multi-colored lights.

He suspected the reason she was crying, but he asked anyway. "What's the problem?"

How could she make him understand how she felt? She tried, "I miss the lights. I miss the red lights and the green lights and the blue lights and the yellow lights." That didn't really explain it all, but it was true. "If I could just see some colored lights, I think I could make it through the holidays."

For once he couldn't think of anything to say to encourage her. He felt the same way, but of course, a real man doesn't cry. He felt like it, but he had to be strong for her sake. He had to get out into the fresh air. After mumbling something about taking his turn outside, he felt his way to the entrance and opened it. There was a little light. He quickly closed the entrance so that she would not freeze before he returned. When he stood up and looked around, he saw that the clouds had disappeared. The northern lights were putting on a most majestic display. There were reds and greens and blues and yellows. He remembered what she had just said about missing the Christmas lights. She wouldn't miss out this Christmas after all. After looking around quickly to be sure there were no polar bears, he hurried back inside.

"It's your turn," he said.

She was still crying. "Why bother? Just let me die here."

"You can't do that. You would miss out on your Christmas present."

"What Christmas present? I suppose you are going to tell me Santa Claus is outside with his sleigh and sack of goodies.

Since we are so close to the North Pole, we should be his first stop."

"Actually, there are a couple settlements farther north, but there is no Santa Claus. If there were, he wouldn't live at the North Pole. It is in the middle of the Arctic Ocean. There is a Christmas present for you though. Go outside and see what Mother Nature has for you."

A minute before, she just wanted to die. Now she had to see what he was talking about. He took off the bearskin coat for her to use. She crawled through the entrance and stood up outside. What was out there that he thought she would want? There was nothing on the ground. Fortunately, it was light enough that she could see around. The last few days it had been completely dark. Wait a minute. Why was it light enough that she could see? She looked up, and then she saw her Christmas present. It was just what she had wished for. Mother Nature had indeed given her the multi-colored lights she wanted. In fact, the lights filled the whole sky. They jumped and danced in a most spectacular display. For a few minutes she forgot about the cold. She forgot about being always hungry. She even forgot about missing her family. Most importantly, she forgot her death wish.

She normally only stayed outside for a couple minutes because of the extreme cold. He usually had to insist that she walk around the igloo a couple times so that her muscles would not atrophy. After ten minute he began to worry. She had seemed suicidal before she went outside. Would she deliberately try to freeze to death? He remembered that he had told her it was one of the most comfortable ways to die. Had that been a mistake? Should he go outside to check on her? She had the coat. He would freeze very quickly without it. He had to see what was wrong.

He opened the entrance and crawled out. She was standing just outside looking up into the sky with a big smile on her face.

Had she frozen in that position? He quickly went to her and asked if she was okay. She turned to him, still smiling.

"Oh, it is so beautiful. Thank you for the best Christmas present ever."

She was okay. He was relieved. "Don't thank me. It is from Mother."

"Who?"

"Mother Nature."

"Oh, yes, it is from Mother Nature." She was so happy she couldn't resist a little tease. "You notice it is Mother, not Father, you male chauvinist."

She was back to normal again after her bout of depression. That was good. She had said she could make it through the holidays if she could see the lights, and she had seen the greatest light show ever. He was freezing, and so was she, even though she didn't notice. He insisted that they go back inside.

The next day was Christmas. As at Thanksgiving their feast consisted of an extra ration of frozen bear meat. They were so hungry it seemed like a meal fit for a king. They had no presents of a material nature to give each other, but they gave what they had. They sang a couple of Christmas carols, and then he reminded her that they had what the people had at the first Christmas. They had hope.

A week later a new year began. Surely this year they would return home.

Chapter 13 The Sun Returns

The encouragement of the holiday season lasted for about a week after the new year. By then the cold, hunger, darkness and apparent endlessness of the winter again took its toll on her nerves. In her weakened condition she was so depressed that she just wanted it all to end even if it meant death.

They had piled about three feet of snow over their little shelter. It was small enough that their body heat kept it a little warmer than the outside. Before winter had set in, they had gathered as much mosses and lichens as they could. That helped too. Still it was so cold that they were concerned about frostbite. They continually warmed their hands and feet by breathing on them or putting them inside their clothes. They also tried to move around to keep their blood circulating. When the temperatures dropped to near zero inside their enclosure, he insisted that they take turns sleeping so that one of them would not freeze to death during the night. She had wanted to completely block off the entrance to stop the cold air from coming in, but he reminded her that they had to have a little fresh air so that they would not be asphyxiated. All this meant that they were alive, but just barely.

He had said that when she couldn't complain anymore, they would be in big trouble. Although he had said that in frustration, he knew there was some truth to it. They often sat in silence for a while when they couldn't think of anything to talk about, but one day he thought she had been quiet for too long.

"Are you okay"?

There was no response. He didn't know if she could hear him or not. Was she asleep, or maybe worse? He tried again.

"Come on, say something."

He took hold of her shoulders and shook her. At first there was nothing. Then in a very weak voice she said, "We're not going to make it." There was a pause, and then she continued, "The winter is never going to end."

"Sure it will. We just need to hang on a little longer." He was worried. She wasn't complaining; she was giving up. What could he do?

"The winter is never going to end." She had already said that. He was really worried now. In all the time they had been together he had never heard her talk like this.

"You have to pull yourself together."

In an even weaker voice she said again, "The winter is never going to end."

She was dying. It was not just the cold or hunger. She had lost all hope. Her mind was going. What could he do? He tried again, "Snap out of it." There was nothing.

He shook her again. She responded by saying, "It's over."

"No, it's not. It's only over if you give up."

She wouldn't say anything else. He shook her again, but to no avail. He had to think of something to do soon, or it *would* be over for her. What could he do? He remembered the time he had nearly frozen to death, and she had kept him conscious by slapping his face. He wasn't in the habit of hitting girls, but their situation was becoming desperate. He gave her a slap. She moaned a little. Then he had another idea. When they had first arrived, she had become animated because she was angry with him. If he could make her angry again, maybe it would give her enough fight to keep going.

"I know I said I wouldn't call you a dumb blond again, but you really are stupid. I guess a girl can't have brains and blond hair both. Why couldn't I have been marooned here with a brunette instead? At least I could have some intelligent conversation.

No, I have to get stuck here with an idiot who gives up on me the first thing. No wonder you are just a worthless waitress; you aren't good for anything else."

He didn't mean a word he was saying, but he looked for some reaction. She made an unintelligible sound that suggested she was becoming irritated. Maybe it was working.

"And another thing, I hate blond hair. I think it is ugly. I think you are ugly. They say beauty is only skin deep, but ugly can go clear to the bone. I never thought that was true until I met you. Now I have the proof of it right in front of me. I'm glad it is dark in here so that I don't have to look at your repulsive face. It is no wonder your parents kicked you out of their house. They probably couldn't stand your disgusting face and bad attitude."

"Oh, you, stop it. They didn't kick me out. I left on my own. What would you know about it anyway? You never met them. They loved me."

In a less belligerent tone he asked, "If that is true, wouldn't you like to see them again?"

"Of course, but why are you being so mean?" She thought for a minute. He had never acted like that before. Then she figured out his trick. "Wait a minute. Wait just one minute. You're not mad at me. You don't mean anything you just said. You just wanted to make me angry so that I wouldn't give up. I'm on to you."

"So, what are you going to do about it?"

She tried to think what she would do. She was angry because he had insulted her, and she was angry because he had tricked her. However, he had done it to save her life. How was she supposed to react? This was all so confusing. She had to get some fresh air.

"Give me that fur coat. I'm not staying in here with such a rude, deceitful male chauvinist, and you are a pig."

She hoped the cold air would help clear her head. It helped some, but mostly it just nipped at every bit of exposed skin. She quickly returned to the relative warmth of the igloo.

"Wow, it's really cold out there. How much longer do you think it will be before it starts warming up? I can hardly wait for spring."

She was looking forward to spring instead of thinking winter would never end. He replied, "Welcome back."

"Did you mean any of those things you said?"

"Not really. The truth is I prefer blonds."

She was embarrassed and wanted to change the subject. "Didn't you say we should be seeing some civil twilight by the middle of January?"

"That's right. It is only about a week away. After that it should only be a couple more weeks before the sun rises again. Since the sun set for the winter a few days after November 5th, it should rise sometime around Groundhog Day. Then the days will rapidly get longer." He didn't mention the fact that the next month would be the coldest part of the winter, and that Resolute had never had a temperature above freezing before May 6.

The long cold winter night continued to drag on. He tried to keep her talking to distract her. If he could get her to focus on the return of sunlight, she would have hope. He knew that February would be the coldest month. Further south the temperatures started to rise in March, but where they were, March was the third coldest month. It was even colder than December. If she knew that, she might give up again. He didn't know if they could survive the cold, but he was sure she wouldn't make it if she lost hope. Then there was the problem of their food supply. It would run out sometime in April. There would be no thawing of the ice until May. Could he cut a hole in the ice to try fishing before all the bear meat was gone? He didn't know, but at least there would be sunlight and more bearable temperatures.

For the time being they just had to try to survive one day at a time. Each day he reminded her that they were one day closer to seeing the sun again. A week later when he went outside for his daily dose of fresh air and exercise, he looked carefully toward the south to see if the sky was any lighter than normal. He was quite sure that it was. Returning to the shelter he gave her the bearskin coat and encouraged her to go outside to see how much lighter it was. Actually, it was only slightly brighter than it had been, but maybe the suggestion that it was getting lighter would make her think it was more than it really was.

She returned to the dark enclosure. He asked, "Well, what do you think? Is it getting lighter?"

"I think so. I can't wait for the sun to peak over the horizon. At least then it will start warming up."

He knew it would be a couple months after the sun rose before there would be any significant warming, but the prospect of warming would encourage her. That was the greatest need for the time being. He felt a little deceitful not telling her how long it would be before temperatures started to rise, but he reasoned that he hadn't actually lied since she hadn't asked when it would warm up. He would try to focus on the increasing daylight and avoid anything that would lead her to ask about the temperatures.

Each day they checked on the light around noon. They could tell that it was definitely getting brighter. After a week there was enough twilight that they could see quite well. Braving the cold he walked to the highest point on the island and looked around. As expected, there was nothing to see but ice and snow. Quickly he returned to their home. She would need the fur coat. At least his walk had warmed him a little.

Perhaps it would help if they could make a game out of predicting the exact day the first ray of sunlight would peak over the horizon. He decided to pick a day earlier than he really thought it would be so that she would not feel like they had a long time to wait. She tried to be sensible. The sun had set a few days after November 5. Since the sun rises at Resolute on February 4, it should rise where they were a few days before then. He had said earlier that the sun would rise by Groundhog Day, which was February 2. She predicted February 1. They would only have to wait a few more days to see who was closest.

One question came to her mind. "What if we are not outside when the sun first peaks out? We could miss the first sunrise."

"You don't have to worry about that. At Resolute on February 4 there is an hour of sunshine."

Really? From nothing to an hour in one day? That's amazing."

"Amazing? The next day there are nearly two hours of sunlight. By the end of February the sun is up for eight and a half hours."

"Wow. That should really warm things up."

"Yes, the sun will definitely warm things up," he said only half honestly. Well, it was true. By April the sun would have warmed things up some.

Each day they checked to see how much lighter it was getting. She was still cold and hungry, but she had something to look forward to now. It would only be a few more days until the sun returned, and then it would get warmer. Fortunately she didn't know how long it would be before it would get warmer. The day he had predicted came without any sun, but it was clear that the sun was very near the horizon. It couldn't be long now.

The last day of January arrived. Would this be the day they would see the sun again? At noon the sky was so bright they were sure they would see a sunbeam any time, but as the minutes passed, they realized it would not be that day.

The next day was the first of February. Would she be right in her prediction? Sure enough, just after noon a beautiful ray of sunlight burst over the horizon through the bitterly cold air. The sun had returned.

Chapter 14 More Sun, But More Cold

It was like Christmas again. The sun was shining, and spring was next month. It had to warm up soon. She stayed outside as long as she could stand the bitter cold. He had already been outside.

When she returned to the darkness of the shelter, she asked if they could find a way to let some of the sunlight in. Of course, they could leave the entrance open, but that would let in the cold air. The previous fall they had used a piece of ice to let in some light, but now the igloo was covered with three feet of snow. There really was no way to let in any light without freezing. It would have been nice if they had some way to make a fire, but that would not be an option for a long time. Maybe when the temperatures rose, they could remove enough snow to expose the piece of ice in the ceiling. Until then they would have to continue to feel around in the dark except when they went outside. That was okay; they knew where everything was by now.

As he had said, the next day had about two hours of sunshine. After that the days continued to get longer. When the sunshine was combined with the twilight, the days soon returned to what seemed like normal lengths.

They were into the coldest part of winter now. Every day was a struggle to keep from freezing to death. Every day they tried to avoid frostbite. They continued to take turns sleeping so that they would not freeze to death while unconscious. That meant that they did not sleep well. Every half hour or so one of them awoke the other. They were always shivering. He reminded her that as long as they shivered, they were surviving. If they stopped shivering in the intense cold, they would die.

He tried to get her to focus on the increasing hours of sunlight. The hope that it would soon warm up was all that kept them going. He also tried to keep her talking. If nothing else, she was getting quite an education about the Arctic and the Eskimos.

"I don't see how the Eskimos could stand to live like this. What did they do all winter?"

"They actually were busy a lot of the time. They hunted seals when they were able to. The dogs had to be fed every other day. That took a lot of meat.

The women had to tend the seal oil lamps they used for heat and light. It was difficult to start a fire, which meant they had to be sure the lamps didn't go out.

Figure 6 Seal Oil Lamp

Sometimes they couldn't go out because of the weather. They learned to be very patient when they had to stay inside their igloos for long periods of time. I read about a white man who lived with the Eskimos for many years. He had just one book to read. Since there was nothing else to do, he read that one book over and over until he almost had it all memorized."

"Wait. Did you say the dogs had to be fed every other day?"

"That's right."

"I don't understand. Why were they so mean? Why wouldn't they let them eat every day?"

"The Eskimos knew what they were doing. They had centuries of experience using their dogs. There was no need to feed them every day. In fact, the dogs were able to pull the sleds better on the second day after they were fed."

"Well, I hope they at least let them inside when it was cold."

"No. The dogs were always outside even when it was 60 below zero."

"That's really cruel. Surely they would freeze to death in such cold."

"The only case I remember of a dog freezing was in Antarctica. It froze standing up. Years later when another explorer came there, the dog was still standing there just as it had been when it froze."

"That's spooky. I can't believe dogs can take so much cold."

"The wild animals don't have any shelter in winter. How do you think they survive?"

"I don't know. It must be hard on them."

"They have survived for centuries. They have thick hides and fat."

She thought for a minute. Then she said, "That reminds me of something you said. When I asked why we couldn't leave this winter, you said we needed food and clothes. I don't see how next winter will be any better than this winter."

"It may not be." He had done it again. That was certainly not something she wanted to hear. Why hadn't he thought before stating the simple truth?

It was obvious that she was near the end of her endurance. The only thing that kept her going was the knowledge that days were getting longer, and it soon would warm up.

"I couldn't stand another winter like this. What makes you think we will be able to leave next year when we can't leave now? We aren't likely to kill another bear. In fact, if one came, it is more likely it would kill us. We aren't doing very well at fishing. It seems to me we will be worse off next winter."

She was right of course. He tried to think how to answer. "The main reason we couldn't leave this year is because we only have one fur coat. One of us would freeze to death. We need each other."

"But that's just it. We might catch some fish, but we have no way to get another fur coat. Like I said, if another bear comes, we will probably be its lunch."

"We certainly need to be on the lookout for bears. However, there is a chance we could do something about our clothes problem. In the spring the birds return to the Arctic. If we can catch some of them, we will have feathers and down for insulation. They can also provide us with eggs and meat."

"But what good is insulation without hides?"

"Actually, Eskimos used the skins of birds and even fish."

"I didn't know fish had skin."

"What do you think the scales attach to?"

"I don't know. Do you really think we can make adequate clothes from bird and fish skins?"

"They might help some. What we really need are seals."

"But you said already there are no seals for a day's walk in any direction."

"Maybe there are none now, but they swim long distances. There are fish here. That is what seals eat. The bear must have thought there was a chance of finding seals here."

"How far do seals swim?"

"They often swim 6000 miles a year. Sometimes they go eight months without ever touching land."

"How can they go that far? They must really swim fast."

"They do. Normally they go about six miles per hour, but they can go up to eighteen miles per hour if they want to."

"Why would they want to?"

"To keep away from polar bears."

"How fast do they swim?"

"Six miles per hour. They can run twenty-five miles per hour. That is why smart seals stay close to the water; dumb ones are lunch."

"We can't swim six miles per hour. How can we catch any seals?"

"They like to sun themselves on land. If we can get between them and the sea, we might be able to kill some."

"I don't want to kill any of them."

"Do you want to stay here another winter?"

"No."

That was the end of the discussion. She didn't want to kill, but she would have to in order to survive and escape the island. Again she asked herself why the real world had to be so cruel.

The bitterly cold days of February dragged on ever so slowly. The days were getting longer. Why was it not getting warmer? She had lived in Chicago where it normally stayed cold through most of the month. Surely, if she could just make it to March, it had to warm up. As he had said, by the end of the month there were nearly nine hours of sunlight every day.

Chapter 15 Spring, But Not Spring

Somehow they managed to survive to the first of March. The lengthening days and hope that it would soon warm up was all that kept them going. She complained a lot, but he didn't mind. He knew that complaining meant surviving. Sometimes he acted more disgusted with her whining than he really was. Of course, by now they knew each other well enough that she was harder to fool. If he said things to make her angry that were clearly not true, she understood. Other times he really was angry. Their circumstances were about as bad as they could be, but why did she have to make things worse with her incessant nagging and bickering?

"I can't stand any more of this cold. Why don't you do something about it?"

"What do you think I can do? I don't control the weather."

"You always think you know everything. Why can't you find some way to help?"

"I've done everything I can. We have a shelter. It is covered with lots of snow. We have mosses and lichens for insulation. There's the bear skin. I don't see what else you expect me to do."

"Why can't we have a fire?"

"You know very well why we can't have a fire. There is no way to start one, and there is no fuel."

"Well, do something about it."

She was being completely unreasonable. He tried to think. Maybe he could get her to refocus on the increasing sunlight.

"Look, we have made it to March. February is the coldest month. Since we survived the coldest part of the winter, we should be able to make it to spring. The first day of spring is just three weeks away. On that day there are twelve hours of sunlight everywhere in the world. The sun sets at the South Pole and rises at the North Pole. It doesn't set again for six months. For those six months there are more hours of sunlight north of us than south of us. Since we are getting nine hours of sunlight now, that means we will gain three more hours in the next three weeks."

"Does that mean it will warm up?"

He knew that it would only be slightly warmer by the end of March. It wouldn't be until April that temperatures rose significantly. Still it would not be an actual lie to say that it would warm by the end of the month. "Yes, it will, but we need to start thinking about what we need to do when spring gets here. We are going to be busy."

"Busy? We have nothing to do but sit here and shiver."

"Maybe there is not much to do now, but we need to plan because there will be lots to do when it warms up."

She tried to think what they could plan for. "I don't get it. What plans are you talking about?"

"Well, first of all, we need to be ready for the first day of spring. That is the day we can measure the angle of the sun at noon."

"What good will that do? We can't change it."

"Of course not, but it will tell us our latitude."

"I thought we already knew that. You said it is 75 degrees north."

"That is true, but we can verify it and maybe get a more accurate reading."

"But how will that help? We are still stuck here. A more accurate reading will not get us off this horrible island."

"I know, but we need to know as much as possible about our location. When we leave here next winter, we will probably find another island. When we do, we can measure again to see how far we have traveled and how far we still have to go. Trust me; I know what I am doing."

"That's a joke if I ever heard one. It's all your fault we ended up here."

"It's because of me we are still living."

"Do you call this living?"

They had had this argument so many times it seemed pointless to repeat it again.

"Look, if you don't like living in my shelter, feel free to go outside."

"What do you mean *my shelter*? I helped build it too. Why don't you go outside? No, don't. I hate you, but you are warm."

"I'd like to go outside. Being stuck in here with you is like living with a porcupine."

"And being with you is like living with a skunk. You stink."

So the fights continued. They certainly were not enjoying each other's company, but they knew they needed each other. When the debate ran out of steam, they were again silent for a while. He returned to his plans for the spring. It seemed like it would never come, but he knew it would. They had to be ready.

The first week of March slowly passed. Then the second week came and went. The days were noticeably longer, but the only way they could tell was by the small hole in the entrance that let in fresh air. Actually, cold air might be a better description. When would it ever warm up? Finally the first day of spring arrived. He made his measurement of the sun's angle at noon. Of course, it just told them what they already knew. The sun was fifteen degrees above the horizon. It verified their latitude, but the main reason he made a big deal about it was so that she would have something to look forward to on that day.

It was still very cold, but there was just a little over a week left of March. In April it would be noticeably warmer. A few days later she was back to complaining again.

"You said it would be warmer in March. The month is almost over, and I can't tell that it is the least bit warmer. There are more hours of sunlight, but I can't see it because it is always dark in here."

"It only warms a little in March, but you will notice a significant improvement next month."

"Will the snow melt then?"

"No, we don't have to worry about that until May."

"Why would we need to worry? I want it to warm up. I can't stand the cold."

"When it warms up, the ice and snow will melt. We will have to remove the snow from our igloo so it doesn't drip down on us and make a mess. We also need to save as much ice as we can."

"Look, Dummy, we are in the Arctic. If there is anything we don't need more of, it is ice."

"I'm not the one who is blond. We need ice to preserve our meat. It will be above freezing for a whole month this summer."

"There you go with that dumb blond stuff again. I'm sick of it."

"You are the one who said *Dummy.*"

He had to think of some way to stop the arguing. She had mentioned that they couldn't see the sunlight because it was always dark in their enclosure. Maybe there was something he could do about that.

"I have an idea. Since it will soon be getter a little warmer, I think I could remove a little snow from the center of our roof. There would still be enough to provide insulation, but some sunlight could get through the piece of ice on the ceiling."

"Okay, I am tired of being in the dark all the time. Go do it."

"Don't get carried away. We need to wait a few more days until it warms up some."

"I'm tired of waiting. I've been waiting all winter for it to warm up. You said it would be warmer in March, and here we are at the end of March, and it hasn't warmed up at all."

"Just hang on. You don't want to freeze to death when there are just a few more days before warmer weather. As I said before, for the next six months there are more hours of sunlight north of us than south of us. Temperatures will start to rise significantly very soon."

"How soon?"

"Very soon."

"Don't give me that. I want to know how soon. Do you mean two or three more months?"

"No, I mean next month."

"Yeah, right. I suppose you mean the end of next month."

"No, I mean it will be warmer the first part of the month, and it will continue to warm through the month."

"Will all the snow melt in April?"

"No, the snow doesn't melt until May."

"I thought you said it will be warmer."

"I did. I said it will be warmer; I didn't say it would be hot."

"How hot does it get here in the summer?"

"The record high temperature for Resolute is 68 degrees."

"That's not very hot."

"We're in the northern Arctic."

"Okay, so when can we get some more light in here?"

"How about the first of April?"

"That had better not be an April Fool's joke."

"It won't be."

Chapter 16 Finally Warmer

The first day of April finally arrived. Now they were getting nearly fourteen hours of sunlight every day. He had said he would remove some snow from their roof to let in some light. She made sure he didn't renege on his promise.

"Okay, Smarty, this is the day you said you would remove the snow from our roof to let in the light. I'm sick and tired of being in the dark all the time. Go do what you promised."

"First of all, last time you called me Dummy. Make up your mind. You can't have it both ways. Second, I didn't say I was going to remove all the snow. We need to keep most of it for insulation for a while."

"Is there a third? It's nice to know you can count."

"Stop it. I have been putting up with you and your constant complaining all winter. I said I would remove some of the snow, and that is what I will do. Hand me that shoulder blade from the bear."

"You're not going to hit me with it, are you?"

"Of course not. Why are you so dumb?"

"I told you I am sick and tired of you calling me a dumb blond all the time."

"I only called you that once, and I said I was sorry."

"What about the time you said you had promised not to call me a dumb blond, but you really thought I was stupid?"

"That didn't count. I just said it to make you angry. I already told you I didn't mean it."

"I thought you just said you didn't mean what you said about not liking blond hair. I distinctly remember you saying, 'The truth is I prefer blonds.'"

"I do."

"I suppose what you really mean is that you prefer a different blond."

"I don't seem to have many others to choose from right now. Now stop this senseless arguing. Do you want some light or not?"

"Of course, but why do you need the shoulder blade?"

"For a shovel of course. Maybe it really is not possible to have blond… no, I'm not going to say it."

"Are you sure you're not going to hit me?"

"Only if I have to. Now, for the last time, hand me the shoulder blade."

She handed it to him. She really didn't think he would hit her, but she couldn't forget the one time he did. He had had a good reason, and if she had been a man, she wouldn't have given it a second thought. However, she was a woman, and she just couldn't forget it.

As he headed outside, he instructed her, "Watch the ceiling. I will just remove a little snow from the center of the roof. We need to keep most of it for insulation. As soon as you notice a little light, tell me."

"Yes, Master."

"Stop the sarcasm."

At least they had something to do to occupy a little of their time, and it would be nice to finally have a little light after all the months of darkness. The temperature had risen some, but it was still below zero. He began shoveling the snow away from the center of the roof.

She was tempted not to tell him when she first saw some light so that she could get more light, but he had the bear skin, and it was still very cold. He normally knew what he was doing, and she didn't want to make him angry by not telling him what he wanted to know. She didn't want him to hit her. Actually, she knew he wouldn't, but in the back of her mind she thought he might. The stress of the last few months was making her imagine things that were just not true.

She called out to him that she could see a little light. At first he didn't hear, but after yelling louder he finally did. He returned and closed off the entrance. Looking around, he said, "Well, it is light enough to see, but there is not much to look at."

"So, I'm not much to look at."

"I wasn't talking about you."

"Well, I'm the only thing here, and you said there's not much to look at."

"Will you stop that?"

"Why can't you be nice to me for a change?"

"Like I said before, being nice to you is like hugging a porcupine."

"A porcupine? Do you have any other great analogies?"

"How about a rattlesnake?"

"A rattlesnake? Okay, thou great mastermind, how am I like a rattlesnake?"

"Just forget it."

"Oh no, your humble slave would like to learn from your great wisdom."

"Okay, you asked for it. A rattlesnake has a pattern on its back and a rattle. It may look interesting, but if you get too close, you find that it has a really mean bite to it."

"Are you saying I look interesting?"

"I was saying you have a mean bite."

"You said yourself I can't have it both ways. If you say I have a mean bite, then you have to admit I am interesting to look at."

"Will you just stop it?" He was getting really tired of her reading into everything he said.

Suddenly her attitude changed. "I'm sorry."

"You are?" he said without thinking. The reversal caught him off guard.

"I know you are not all bad."

He was tempted to ask her estimate of the approximate amount, but after speaking without adequate thought, he decided to hold his tongue for the time being.

She remembered how he had kept her from freezing that first night. He had helped her find water to drink. It was his plan that had enabled them to catch some fish to keep from starving. He had risked his life to make the spear that had made it possible to kill the bear. He had kept her from giving up so that they could make it to spring. Now he had made it possible to have some light in their home. Spring was returning, and all she did was complain. She felt guilty that she didn't show more appreciation. She concluded, "You're really not bad at all."

That was quite an improvement. He had gone from somewhat less than bad to zero percent bad in just less than a minute. He wondered how long it would be before he was a hundred percent bad again. He was sure it wouldn't be long. He was careful not to say anything because he knew that anything he said could and would be used against him not only in the very near future but repeatedly as long as they both should live. Was he being too cynical?

She continued, "I know I must look like a mess." With that she began to cry.

Why do women always have to do that? He looked at her. He hadn't really seen her for some time. It had been dark in their shelter all winter, and they didn't go outside at the same time because they only had one coat. Both of them had lost a lot of weight. Half of her hair was cut short. She hadn't washed her face for months, and her makeup was long gone. The cold, hunger and depression had taken its toll on her appearance. She looked years older than she was. He remembered how nice she had looked in her waitress's outfit the first time he had seen her on the plane. Then he had seen the fear in her eyes, and he instinctively felt he had to do what he could to protect her. Seeing her now made him feel sorry for her. Since he couldn't shave, his beard had grown and covered much of his face. Men don't care what they look like, but he knew that a woman's appearance was important to her sense of self-esteem. What could he say? As a journalist he believed in telling the truth even if it hurt. However, he knew her feelings were very fragile right now. He couldn't say she looked beautiful because it just wasn't true, and she knew it. He had to say something. "It is true you don't look all that great right now, but it is only temporary. We will get through this. Spring is here. We will have warmer weather and more to eat. We'll get back home. Just hang on."

"Do you really think we can make it back to civilization?"

"Yes, I do. Things are looking up for us now. This is not the time to give up." He didn't feel completely confident they would get back home, but they did have a reasonable chance.

As the days went by, temperatures continued to rise. That is not to say it was warm; it was still very cold. It just was not as bitterly cold as it had been. In another month they would finally see some thawing. After a couple weeks, while he was marking their calendar, he noted that it was April 15. He asked her, "Do you know what day this is?"

"The fifteenth, why?"

"Don't you know what is special about that date?"

"It is the middle of April. Is there something else?"

"It's tax day. This is the day everyone in America is supposed to have his taxes filed. Do you see how lucky we are? They say the two things in life that are sure are death and taxes. We don't have to worry about taxes."

"Oh, great. We have so many advantages I can barely contain myself. We are in danger of dying from a half dozen or more things, but we don't have to pay taxes. Like I said at the beginning, we must be the luckiest people in the whole world. Why don't you go outside and see if there is an IRS agent waiting at the door of our mansion?"

"It is more likely there would be a polar bear. I suppose in a way that is similar. They both want to get everything out of us they can."

"Now who is being cynical? How about scraping some more snow off our roof? I would like more light."

"I guess it is warm enough now. I will scrape away the snow down to the piece of ice."

With that he went outside and did as he said. It made it brighter in the shelter. The sun was shining for nearly eighteen hours a day now. With the civil twilight it was never really dark anymore. In a little over two weeks the sun would not set at all. Temperatures had risen enough that they no longer were concerned about freezing while asleep. That meant they could sleep at the same time.

Getting more restful sleep helped their dispositions, but the next problem they faced was food. Their supply of bear meat was getting very low. The ice would not start to melt for another month. If they couldn't catch some fish before then, they would starve. He went out to the sea and looked around. The rise and fall of the tides was continually breaking the ice.

With the cold temperatures the exposed water froze quickly. Now that it was a little warmer, it took longer for it to freeze. If he could break up the ice by one of the cracks, maybe he could try fishing again. How could he break the ice? An ax would help. What did the Eskimos use for an ax? Of course, bones. The leg bones of the bear would work for handles, and they had lots of stones. The gut from the bear would hold the ax head to the handle. He had a plan.

When he explained it to her, she agreed. She was glad they didn't have to use any more of her hair. It was good he had the foresight to save the intestines. They spent the rest of the day making the ax. By then they were tired and decided to wait until the next day to try it out. Both of them were weak from lack of food.

The next morning he went to the shore and looked for a place where the ice was cracked, and the surrounding ice seemed thin enough that he could chop through it. It took a long time, and in his weakened condition he had to rest frequently, but he was able to make a hole big enough to put down his net. He tried fishing for a while without success. He was tired, and he knew she would be cold without the bearskin. Returning to the shelter, he told her that he had been able to make a hole, and he had seen some fish.

The next day he returned to the hole. Some ice had formed, but it didn't take long to remove it. He had learned the previous fall how to catch fish. It was different fishing through a hole in the ice, but after a couple hours, he was able to catch a medium size fish. He ran back to their home and announced, "I've got great news. It's feast day."

"You caught a fish. That's wonderful. I am so tired of eating nothing but bear meat, and the best thing is that it isn't even frozen."

"I could put it on ice for a few hours."

"Don't you dare. You're not funny. Can we eat it all now?"

"I think so. We should be able to continue to catch fish now that the weather is getting warmer."

With that they proceeded to devour the fish. She didn't think to complain that they had to eat it raw. By now eating uncooked meat seemed normal.

Over the next few days he continued to fish. He didn't get one every day, but he was successful enough that they were not starving. The thought occurred to him that there might be bigger fish in the deeper water. The previous fall they had little choice where they could fish because they had to stay on shore. Now the sea was covered with ice. That meant they could go anywhere to try their luck. He went to a spot he thought might be good and chopped another hole. The noise attracted the attention of the fish, and when a big one swam close to the surface, he was able to spear it. For the first time since their arrival they had all they needed to eat. Things were indeed looking up. They had adequate food, and it was finally warmer.

Chapter 17 The Refrigerator

Now that starvation was likely put off until the next winter, he focused his attention on their next problem. They were glad that it was getting warmer, but that meant new challenges. In May the ice and snow would begin to melt. They would not be able to go beyond the shore. The precipitation was so little that they could run short of drinking water. Also, if they were able to get more meat than they needed, they would need to preserve some for the next winter. The temperatures in mid-summer would only be in the forties, but that was warm enough that meat could spoil. What they needed was a refrigerator.

She could tell he was thinking again. "Okay, I know you are up to something. It had better not cost me any more hair. My stylist will have enough trouble when I go in for my next perm."

"Don't worry. I don't need you; I have bear gut."

She wasn't sure if she should be angry or amused. Apparently, he was trying to be funny. She was tired of fighting, and things had improved some. Maybe it would be better to play along. "So now I am lower than an animal's intestines."

"I didn't say that. I was just pointing out that we probably won't have to use your hair anymore."

"Can I have my hair back then?"

"I don't think you can reattach it."

"I know. So what are you thinking about that will be gut-wrenching for the bear but won't cost me?"

"We need a refrigerator."

"Oh, is that all? Why didn't you say so? Let's just go downtown and buy one."

"I don't think they have the model I prefer."

"Well, that should not be a problem for someone as smart as you. Just order the one you want, and the next plane going to Resolute can drop it off on the way through."

"Logically, if a plane could drop off a refrigerator, it could pick us up and get us back home."

"Well, gee-whiz, why didn't I think of that? You are so brilliant."

"Can't we ever have a conversation without you being sarcastic?"

"Well, you are the one who thinks he can buy a refrigerator."

"I didn't say we could buy a refrigerator. I said we need a refrigerator."

"Okay, I know I am just a dumb blond. I couldn't possibly be as smart as you. I will just shut up and do as I am told. I'm sure you have a great plan because you are so much wiser than I am. How are we going to get a refrigerator?"

"Will you stop that? I am not trying to demean your intelligence. I am just pointing out that we need to find a way to keep things cool."

"I know you are going to try to make me look foolish, but I would like to point out that we are in the Arctic. There is ice and snow everywhere we look. Could you explain to me why we need to keep things cool?"

"In July temperatures could get over fifty degrees. Since summer is when we are likely to find the most food, we need to be able to preserve it."

"But what if we don't have extra food?"

"Then we won't need to keep it from spoiling, but we don't know how much we will be able to get. We can't wait until we have the meat to prepare. By then the ice will all be melted. We must save ice now."

"Okay, but it seems like a lot of work for something we may not need."

"It is better to have the ice and not use it than to need it and not have it."

"I understand. So what is your plan?"

"Let's make another ax. We have more bones and lots of stones. We can both chop out blocks of ice and transport them to a north facing location. When we have enough ice, we can cover it with rocks. That should keep it from all melting before colder weather comes in September."

"What difference does it make if we put the ice in a north facing place? I thought you said the sun shines all day in the summer."

"It does, but the sun is lower in the sky around midnight. In July the daytime temperatures are in the forties, but the nighttime temperatures are in the thirties."

With that they set to work. Having made one ax, they were able to make another without much trouble. Over the next few days they alternated between fishing and moving ice to their "refrigerator". The first week of May the sun stopped dipping below the horizon at night. His next concern was to remove the rest of the snow from their home before it began to melt. Rather than throw it off and leave it, he insisted on taking it to the location where they had found water the previous fall. With only about six inches of precipitation all year he knew they might run out of drinkable water before the summer was over. The holes they made from removing ice provided more fishing locations. That meant that they were getting enough fish to eat, but there was no extra. Soon the ice would melt for the summer. What would they do then? They would have a hard time catching enough for their current needs. How could they hope to get more to save for the winter? She was concerned.

"I don't see how we are going to make it. We are just getting enough to eat for now. Fishing is not likely to improve. I wonder if we gathered all that ice for nothing."

"We won't get enough fish to survive."

"Do you mean we will die?"

"Not necessarily. We just won't catch enough fish to make it."

"But fish are all we have to eat. We are not likely to kill another bear."

"I agree."

"There you go again. You are contradicting yourself. You say we won't get enough fish to survive, and we have nothing else to eat. How can we survive?"

"I didn't say we have nothing else to eat. I just agreed we are not likely to kill another bear."

"Look around you, Bozo. Fish are all we have. Do you think we can eat rocks?"

"They might be a little too crunchy for my palate. However, the rocks are where we should look to supplement our diet."

"Are you going to make another remark about my hair color and IQ?"

"I didn't say anything about either."

"Well, stop baiting me. How are we going to supplement our diet with rocks?"

"Just wait another two or three weeks, and you will see."

"I don't want to wait two or three weeks. If you know something, tell me."

He could see that she was getting angry. It was tempting to keep playing his game, but maybe it would be best to explain. They would have to be together for a long time yet.

"Okay, I can say it all in one word."

"Well, fine. What is the word?"

"Birds."

"Birds? In case you haven't noticed, there are no birds here."

"There are only a few birds that stay in the Arctic all winter. Most of them are farther south. However, in late May many migratory birds return to the north. The Arctic tern goes all the way to the northernmost Arctic islands. The snow goose also nests as far north as we are. The most common bird in the far north is the ptarmigan. In fact it is the official bird of Nunavut. In late May and early June all these birds and more are laying their eggs. That means we can gather their eggs and catch some of them. I hope we can get some geese. They have valuable down that we can use for insulation."

"I see. Why couldn't you just explain that in the beginning instead of stringing me along?"

"I just thought it would be fun."

"Well, it's not fun for me. You always want to have fun at my expense."

"We don't have a TV. Watching you get angry is the only entertainment I have."

"Oh, just stop it. What do we have to do to catch some birds?"

With that they began to make plans to build traps. The fish net could be used with bones to make a snare to catch birds on their nests. It would be hard to get any of them while in flight, but maybe by working together they could kill some while they were taking off. They looked around the island to see if there was evidence of a nest that had been used before since birds often use the same nests as they did in the past. The birds would soon return, and they would be ready. Hopefully, they would soon have meat to store in their refrigerator.

Chapter 18 Seals

Just as he had said, the last week of May the first birds began to arrive. It wasn't long before they were laying their eggs. They tried to keep a low profile at first so that they would not scare the birds away. Then after a few eggs had been laid, they began snitching some. It was nice to have something to eat besides meat. They decided to wait until most of the egg laying was over before attempting to kill any birds. Then they put their traps to work. It wasn't long before they were getting more meat than they needed for their immediate needs. They put the extra meat into the ice storage. They were making progress, but the amount of meat they were preserving was not nearly enough to feed them through the coming winter.

By late June the ice was melting rapidly. It wouldn't be long before they were surrounded again by open water. They spent most of their time catching birds and fish. It didn't make much difference what time of day they worked or slept since it was light all the time. It was a little warmer in the afternoon than at night because the sun was higher at that time. They put a rock over the hole in the ceiling when they wanted to sleep to make it darker. He reminded her that she had said the previous winter that she wouldn't complain about the sun being in her eyes all the time.

Figure 7 Seals on the Ice

One day as they were resting he thought he heard something that sounded like a dog barking. What could it be? They listened carefully. It was coming from the beach. He warned her to be very quiet and crawled outside. Peeking over the rocks, he saw what he had been hoping for. Seals! This was their best hope to escape the island and survive the next winter. Quickly returning, he whispered to her, "It's a pod of seals."

"It's what?"

"A pod of seals."

"A what of seals?"

"A pod."

"Pods are for peas."

"Pod is the most common term for a group of seals. It can also be called a colony, a crash, a harem, a herd, a rookery, a spring, a team, a flock or a bob."

"What about a pack?"

"No, it's not called a pack."

"Why can't it be called a pack if it is called everything else?"

"I don't know; it just isn't called a pack. Look, we don't have time to debate. This is our big chance to kill enough seals to get the clothes and meat we need to leave the island."

"I don't want to kill seals."

"We have to if we want to survive and get back home. I hope you are not going to wimp out on me. I need your help."

She thought for a minute. The idea of killing seals was repulsive to her, but she realized that it had to be done. Reluctantly she agreed to help. "Okay, what do I have to do?"

"Take your ax. I will use my ax and spear. Stay low behind the shelter. I will circle around and come in from the other side. When I give you the signal, we will both run along the shore to cut off their escape into the water. Then we need to kill as many as we can. This may be our only chance, and we really need their fur and meat. Remember, try to hit them as hard as you can right between the eyes."

"Oh, I wish I didn't have to do this."

"I know, but we have to. Be brave; I need you."

"Okay, I'll do my best."

With that he quietly left the igloo and made a wide circle around the seals. When he got to the shore on the other side, he slowly inched his way along keeping out of sight behind some rocks. He looked toward the shelter and saw her crouched down waiting for him. They would not be able to get any closer without being seen by the seals. It was now or never. He signaled to her, and then jumping up he ran along the shore toward their unsuspecting victims. She did the same.

The seals saw them and instinctively headed for the safety of the water. He reached their escape path just as the first seal slipped into the sea. He began hitting them ferociously. She arrived then and tried to strike a large bull, but it knocked her down and escaped. She tried again, but the next one was past her before she could get in a good blow. The ax hit on its back without doing serious damage. It was gone. Then a cow with a pup beside her was just ahead of her. She was determined she would do the best she could. Gritting her teeth, she stepped in front of the seal and slammed the ax down on its head with all her strength. The seal went down unconscious. The pup had been following its mother, and when she stopped, it stopped beside her. With another blow the baby was dead too.

In the meantime he had been busy. One seal after another fell to his ax. As the last of the pod entered the water, he grabbed his spear and thrust in into the back of the slowest escapee. It was not a fatal blow, but the spear stuck fast. He held on tenaciously. It was an older cow and weighted about as much as he did. At first he wasn't sure what to do. If he let go of the spear, the seal would get away, and he would lose his precious weapon. If he just held on, the seal would not die. Inching his way along the shaft of the spear, he got to the body of his prey. Putting his arms around it, he tried to pick it up and carry it to the land. It wasn't easy because the seal was heavy, and it continued to flop around violently.

He called to her to bring her ax. While he tried to hold the seal still, she attempted to hit it on the head. She nearly hit him instead a few times, but finally she succeeded in getting in a couple good blows on the animal's head. It went limp. He then pulled it the rest of the way onto the land. Taking his own ax, he hit it again a few times to be sure it was dead. Then he went around to all the other seals to make sure they were dead and not just unconscious.

While he was doing that, she returned to the ones she had killed. When he got to her, he found her kneeling beside them weeping.

"What's wrong?" he asked.

"I killed the pup. It didn't want to leave its mother, and I killed it. It was just a poor, helpless baby."

What should he say? Being able to bag these seals was the best thing that had happened since he had killed the bear. She should be jumping for joy instead of crying. Then he remembered how he had spoken out of turn at that time. Perhaps this would be a time to show some sympathy. "I know it was hard for you, but it had to be done. You did well. These seals will make it possible for us to leave the island when the ocean freezes. In another three or four months we might be home again."

"Do you really think so?"

"We can't be sure, but it is possible."

He needed to distract her so that she wouldn't dwell on the killing of the pup.

"We are really lucky to get so many seals, but now we have lots of work to do. The meat needs to be put on ice. If you will check to be sure all of them are dead, I will take the pup to the storage. The first in will be the last out. I want to save the pup until last."

"Why is that?"

"I am thinking of the danger from polar bears. When we leave here, we may be followed by them. If one gets too close, we can leave the seal for it to eat. That way we might be able to escape while it is eating."

"You are always thinking ahead. That's great. I hope we don't see any more bears."

"I hope not too, but we need to be prepared."

With that he picked up the baby seal and headed for the ice storage while she checked the other seals. Of course, he had already made sure they were dead, but giving her that job would keep her busy so that she would not be thinking about the pup. Also, he wanted to get the baby out of her sight. It took a little time to remove the rocks covering the ice. Then he moved some blocks of ice and put the pup as far back in the storage as he could. Returning to the shore, he found her sitting beside the cow she had killed. This was not good.

"Were any of them still alive?" he asked, even though he knew the answer.

"No," was her only reply.

"Okay, we need to get busy. With so much meat we need to work fast so that some of it doesn't spoil before we can get it into storage."

She was still feeling sad about having to kill the mother and baby, but she knew he was right. They needed the meat and the furs. Even though it was the middle of the summer, it was still cold. Temperatures at night were only in the thirties. He had pointed out earlier that the main reason they couldn't leave the island was because they didn't have adequate clothing. Now they had seal skins. They could make mukluks and coats. Maybe they could be home before Christmas. The thought brought her some cheer.

"Okay, tell me what I need to do."

"I thought you didn't like to be told what to do."

"I just don't like being bossed around. You could be polite."

"I'll keep that in mind. Let's start with the bigger bulls. A couple of them must weigh over three hundred pounds. We can't drag them to the storage. Let's cut them up. You hold them in place while I try gutting them."

"You didn't say *please*."

"Okay, please."

"That's better."

They set to work. It wasn't easy. All they had to work with was the spear and a knife they had made from the bones of the bear. In all there were eight seals. He had killed six in addition to the two she had killed. About half of them were too heavy to drag to the storage. After working for a few hours she was getting exhausted. He suggested that she go back to their home to rest. Actually, a big part of the reason he wanted her to leave was so that he could drag her cow away without her watching. He thought it might disturb her.

He continued to work. The Eskimos often worked two or three days straight without rest in the summer when there was a lot that needed to be done. Then they would sleep so soundly that they couldn't be awakened. He kept reminding himself of that as he became more and more weary.

After she had rested a couple hours, she returned to see how he was doing. She noticed that her cow was gone. Then she realized that he had removed it so that she wouldn't see it. She didn't say anything, but she understood that he really did care about her feelings.

"I think I am rested enough to help now. Don't you want a break?"

"I am getting tired, but it is important to get all the meat on ice as soon as we can."

"But it must be close to midnight. The sun is low and about due north. Surely with temperatures in the thirties the meat won't spoil before morning."

"Maybe not, but we want to be sure the birds don't get to it."

112

"They can't eat very much in a few hours."

"That's true, but we don't want them to poke holes in the hides."

"I see. What should I do?"

"There are just a couple more to go. I think if I can cut a little more off this one, the two of us can pull it to the storage. Then we can bring the last one to the shelter and get something to eat."

They did as he suggested. When they got to the igloo, they were both very tired. He reminded her that seal liver was one of the favorite foods of the Eskimos. This was the first time either of them had tasted it. When they had eaten, he asked her what she thought of the taste.

"Well, it's better than frozen, raw, bear meat, but I really would like it cooked."

"Be patient. Maybe someday we can start a fire."

With that they decided it was time for some rest. When they awoke the next day, it was already mid-afternoon. It didn't really matter since the sun was shining all night, but they needed to make sure they recorded the days correctly.

After eating their breakfast (if that is what you call it when eaten in the afternoon), they discussed their next priority.

"You said you know how to sew. Making clothes is our main need now. Do you think you can make a waterproof seam like the Eskimo women?"

"I think so. Just don't ask me to chew hides."

"Okay, but you may wish you had when you see how stiff they can be."

"I just want them to be warm. I'm still cold most of the time."

Over the next weeks she spent most of her time sewing. He mostly fished. By late July the sun was getting closer to the horizon at midnight. The days of twenty-four sun would soon be gone.

Chapter 19 Get Ready to Go

The short Arctic summer would soon be coming to an end. With the possibility of returning home soon within reach, they were both encouraged. What would they need to leave the island? The main concern had been clothes. She had worked diligently to make mukluks, parkas, mittens and hoods. He was glad to have them because she had been wearing the polar bear coat. They both agreed to let her have it because she was always the one who was the coldest. With temperatures in the forties it was bearable but still cool. Putting on the mukluks and trousers, he headed for the shore to try them out. He wanted to see if they were waterproof. He waded into the water up to his waist and stood there for a couple minutes. Then he started to feel moisture in two spots. Returning to the shelter where she was working, he told her where the leaks were.

"Well, I tried to do the best I could. I'm not an Eskimo woman you know."

"Actually, I think you did quite well for your first attempt."

"It would help if I had a better needle than this bear bone."

"I know, but we don't have any walrus tusk."

"I was thinking of a metal needle."

"The Eskimos didn't have metal needles."

"I told you I'm not an Eskimo."

"Well then, next time you are abducted and taken to the Arctic be sure to bring some metal needles along."

"You're not funny. Besides, if I knew I was going to be taken to the Arctic, I think I would take along some matches. I really wish we could make a fire."

"We are getting closer. We have seal oil. All we need is a lamp and some way to get the fire started."

"You're so smart. Why can't you think of some way to make a fire?"

"Intelligence doesn't make a fire. It requires a spark and dry combustible material."

"Can't we just rub two sticks together?"

"We only have one, and I am not going to lose my spear to make a fire."

"I suppose you're right, but I really wish we had fire. I could almost be content if we just had heat, light and a way to cook."

"Be patient. The time may come. For now let's do what we can. How about trying to tighten the seams on these clothes?"

"Okay, I'll try. Is there anything else we need to complete our wardrobe?"

"There is one thing I wish we had."

"What is that?"

"A wolverine."

"I know I will probably regret asking, but why do you wish we had a wolverine?"

"Fur."

"Could you consider speaking in complete sentences? It is quite common in English you know."

"Okay, try this: I wish we had wolverine fur."

"That's not much better than your previous monosyllabic utterance."

"'Monosyllabic utterance'. Wow, those are awfully big words for such a small girl."

"Oh, stop it. You better not say anything about my hair color and intelligence."

"I didn't say anything."

"I know what you're thinking."

He began to laugh. At first she was a bit angry, but then she began to laugh too. Their circumstances had improved a great deal since the winter, and the prospects of returning home had put them in a much better mood. After a good laugh she returned to the question he had raised.

Okay, why do you want wolverine fur?"

"It is the best fur for the hoods of parkas. It doesn't frost up like other furs."

"Why not?"

"It is because of the structure of the hairs. They are smoother than other furs. Moisture tends to form what they call rime ice instead of structural ice. Rime ice is finer and lighter. It can be brushed off more easily and doesn't weigh down the hood."

"Okay, so then, where do we get wolverine fur?"

"From a wolverine."

"Obviously, but where do we get a wolverine?"

"Wherever they live. There are none here. If we make it to the mainland, we might find some. Of course, if we get there, we won't need them because we will be back in civilization."

"Are there any other furs that would work?"

"Wolf and coyote furs are a good second choice."

"We don't have either of them."

"Polar bear fur is probably the best choice we have. As always, we will have to make do with what we've got."

With that she went back to work. Standing in the water to test the trousers and mukluks gave him an idea. Why not stand in the water and cast a net to catch fish? The net they had made from her hair had kept them from starving, but it was rather small. Now that they had adequate hides and seal gut, he could make a larger net. Then he could catch more fish. He went to work.

As he made the net, he was thinking about what else they would need to leave the island. They had enough meat to last through the winter, but they would not be able to carry all of it. They needed a way to carry everything they had. If they could be assured of finding an inhabited island within a week or two, they could carry enough on their backs, but there was no guarantee that they would be so fortunate.

They needed a sled. How could he make one? Once again he thought about what they had available. They would need runners and something for a frame. He remembered reading about some Eskimos making a sled out of frozen meat. It would thaw when the temperatures rose, but until then it would be quite strong. Then he remembered how that story ended. The dogs got loose and ate the meat. Then they ran away. That meant disaster for the Eskimos. He decided not to use meat. They had lots of bones from the bear and the seals. The ribs might work for runners and the larger bones could form a frame. After completing the net he would start on the sled.

The days of August passed quickly. Before they knew it, September arrived. The temperatures were starting to drop, but that was good news. It meant they were getting closer to the time they could leave. One day late in the month he was marking the calendar when he noticed something. Looking over at her he said, "Happy anniversary."

"What are you talking about? We don't have an anniversary."

"Sure we do. It was one year ago today we arrived here. We have succeeded in thwarting the boss's plan to kill us for a whole year. Wouldn't he be surprised if he knew we were still alive? Not only that, but when we arrived, all we had was the clothes we were wearing. Now we have a home, plenty of food, warm clothes and tools and weapons."

"Oh, great! We've got it so good maybe we should just stay here forever. Look, all I care about is getting away from this horrible prison."

"Don't worry. We will be able to leave as soon as the sea freezes over. It should only be about another month. With so many islands out there we should run into one in a week or so. There is just one more thing I can think of that we need to do to prepare."

"Okay, what is it going to cost me this time?"

"Effort."

"I told you before. You need to learn to speak in complete sentences."

"You just asked what it would cost you. What it will cost you is effort. We need to get some exercise. We will be doing a lot of walking, and we need to get in shape."

They had been busy all summer fishing and sewing, but they had had little exercise. They started to walk around the island every day. The entire trip was only about a mile. If they didn't find another island right away, they might have to walk all the way to the mainland 500 miles away. At first the one-mile walks tired them, but after a few days they were able to walk around the island twice a day. Then they increased it to three times. Soon they were able to circle the island five times without becoming overly tired. They were becoming bored with the scenery, but they were looking forward to the time in the near future when they could finally start their journey back to civilization.

Chapter 20 There's No Place Like Home

October arrived. The days were getting shorter again. In another month the long polar night would begin. Temperatures were again in the teens. Unlike the previous year, they were glad to see the colder weather come. It meant the sea would freeze over, and they could finally leave the island that had been both their home and their prison.

Ice crystals were forming on the surface of the ocean. It would only be a few more days before the whole Arctic Ocean was covered with ice. They waited impatiently. Then he thought of something that bothered him. She could tell he was worried.

"I've seen that look before. What's wrong?"

"I wonder if we should wait until spring to leave."

"What? Are you out of your mind? We have been waiting for over a year to get off this awful pile of rocks. Now you want to go through another miserable winter here. I couldn't stand going through what I did last time. How could you even consider staying here any longer?"

"In a few days the sun will set for the winter. I don't want to travel in the dark."

"Surely a big strong man like you isn't afraid of the dark."

"I'm not afraid of the dark. I'm afraid of what might be in the dark."

"There's no such thing as a bogey man."

"That's true, but there is such a thing as a polar bear."

"We haven't seen a polar bear for a whole year, and there are just as many in the day as in the night."

"That's true, but we can see them in the day. We can't at night."

"Well, if we can't see them, they can't see us."

"They can't see us, but they can smell us. Polar bears can see and hear about the same as humans, but they can smell people twenty miles away."

"Couldn't they smell us twenty miles away in the spring?"

"Yes, but we could see them when they were two or three miles away. Then we might be able to keep away from them. At night we wouldn't know a bear was near until it was too late."

"But what good would it do if we could see them? You said before that they run twenty-five miles per hour."

"We can't outrun them, but we can out-walk them."

"That doesn't make any sense. Running is faster than walking."

"That's why we should walk. A bear normally walks about three and a half miles per hour. We can walk faster than that if we are not pulling a sled."

"But we will be pulling a sled."

"If we had to, we could leave it."

"Okay, but I don't want to stay here another winter. You said we could be back in civilization in a couple weeks."

"I said that could happen. There is no guarantee."

"Well, I want to leave. I can't stand it here any longer."

With that the conversation ended. He had some misgivings about leaving when the sun was about to set for the winter, but maybe they would be lucky and find an inhabited island in a few days. He certainly did not relish the idea of spending another winter in that cold, dark shelter. Another reason he was willing to go against his better judgment was that he didn't want to put up with three more months of her constant complaining. He could understand why she was miserable sitting there all winter, but what good did it do to complain all the time? Anyway, when she started complaining about pulling the sled over the ice, he could remind her that it was her idea to leave sooner that he thought wise. For better or worse, the decision was made; they would leave as soon as the ice would hold them.

Figure 8 Loading the Sled

A few days later he decided it was safe to go. They loaded the sled with meat. They also made two backpacks to carry. His was about fifty pounds, and hers was about thirty. They thought that was about what they could each carry without becoming exhausted too soon. Then they took the sled down to the shore so that it would be ready when it was time to go in the morning.

In the morning they got up before sunrise so that they could leave as soon as it was light. They ate a big meal, and then he walked to the highest point on the island to see if there were any bears or anything else of interest. There was nothing but ice.

Returning to the sled, he found her waiting. They each took hold of the bear gut ropes and began pulling the sled onto the ice. They were leaving.

The island had been their home for over a year. After going a couple hundred feet, they stopped to rest and readjust everything. Pulling the sled was harder than they had thought. As they rested, she looked back at the island. She had hated the island all the time they had been there, but now that they were leaving, she didn't want to go. It had been her idea to depart before spring. She had experienced fear, hunger, cold and danger on that pitiful little island, but still it was home. Should they stay? No. She didn't know what lay ahead, but they had to go.

He saw her looking back at the island and surmised what she was thinking. He was less sentimental than she was, but still, there is something about home that draws us back. Should he insist that they return? It was questionable if they should be leaving at this time. No, the decision had been made. They would go on.

Besides, the island really was not their home. His home was in Chicago, and hers was in Vancouver. They must think about their true homes. That was where their loved ones were. That was where they belonged. Picking up the ropes, he said simply, "Come on, let's go home."

Chapter 21 Ice

They took hold of the ropes again and pulled. It was hard going because the sled was heavy, and the ice was not as smooth as they had expected. How could ice be so slippery for them, but not for the sled? Even though they had been exercising every day, they still had to stop to rest every few hundred feet. By the time the sun was setting in the mid-afternoon they were still within sight of the island. This was not going to be as easy as they had expected.

They looked back at the island and then at each other. Each of them knew what the other was thinking. Should they return to the island? They had the means to survive the winter. If they waited until spring, there would be more hours per day of sunlight. Also, by spring more of their meat would be eaten, and the sled would be easier to pull.

He asked, "Do you want to go back?"

She had been insistent about leaving, but now she hesitated. She looked back at the island and then ahead at the endless expanse of ice. Was she being sensible or just headstrong in wanting to go forward? Neither alternative she faced was to her liking. Finally she answered, "No, let's keep going. There are two places I never want to see again. One is Chicago, and the other is that island."

He was not sure if he liked her decision or not. The way ahead would be hard but returning to the island was not much better. There was one difference though between his wishes and hers. Chicago was his home. That was where he wanted to go. At least they agreed that they would continue moving forward.

It was not really late in the day, but the sun was setting. They didn't want to travel in the dark. Not only would they not be able to see polar bears, but they also could not see the unevenness of the ice. That could be dangerous because they could slip or they could break through the ice where it was thin.

They had hoped to build a snow igloo to stay in overnight. That was what the Eskimos normally did when they were on a journey. However, there is little precipitation in the Arctic, and it was still early in the winter season. Maybe that was another reason they should have stayed until spring. Whether their decision was wise or not, they were going forward.

Since they had stopped for the night, they needed to make some kind of shelter. Temperatures at night were already getting close to zero. Without snow to make an igloo, all they could do was to spread sealskins over their sled and anchor them with frozen pieces of meat. Fortunately, there was little wind. After making their little tent, they settled down to a meal of frozen, raw seal meat and fish. At least it was better than bear meat.

It was still early to go to sleep. They talked about their first day off the island.

She remarked, "I didn't realize how hard it would be to pull the sled. At the rate we are going we'll never get to the mainland."

"Your statement is illogical. We are travelling at a finite speed. The mainland is a finite distance away. Therefore, it cannot take an infinite amount of time to get there."

"Thank you for your analysis, Mr. Spock. I can't tell you how helpful you are."

"Of course you can't. Helpfulness is not quantifiable."

"Will you stop that? I just want to know how long it will take to get to our destination."

"I thought you had already determined that it would take infinite time."

"Oh, come on. You know I didn't mean it literally. Why do you always have to be so irritating?"

"Me? What about you? Besides, like I said before, we don't have TV."

"I hope we find an inhabited island soon. I've had about all I can stand of your attitude."

"*I* hope we find an inhabited island soon. I've had about all I can stand of *your* attitude."

"I just said that."

"So did I. At least there is something we agree on."

"Stop it. Just stop it. How long will it take to get to the mainland if we don't find another island?"

"There are many variables that could affect the required time, but if my estimate is correct, and we have traveled about three miles today, we simply need to divide the 500 miles by three. That comes out to 167 days."

"167 days! That is nearly half a year."

"Half a year is 183 days."

"Well, that's close. Isn't there something we could do to speed things up?"

"We could abandon the sled."

"Yes, but then we wouldn't have much to eat."

"Very perceptive."

"We had better find another island soon, or there may be a case of manslaughter, and I do mean MAN-slaughter."

"I wonder why there is such a thing as manslaughter but not woman slaughter."

"Chauvinism. Pure chauvinism."

They were not really as angry with each other as they acted. They simply had gotten into the habit of arguing. It was hard to break old habits.

She still wondered if there was any way to speed up their progress. "You said we could go faster if we abandoned the sled. Isn't there anything else we could do?"

"We could find a way to make it easier to pull."

"Okay, but how could we do that? Did the Eskimos have a way to make it easier to pull a sled?"

"Yes."

"Well, fine. Tell me."

"You might not like it."

"Is this going to cost me more hair?"

"No, it's worse than that."

"What is worse than losing more hair?"

"Ice."

"There you go again with another one-word answer. Explain what you mean."

"We could ice the runners on the sled."

"How is that worse than taking more of my hair?"

"It is the kind of ice that you might object to."

"Ice is ice. What kind of ice are you talking about?"

"Urine."

"What?"

"I said urine. That is the kind of ice we need."

"You are really gross. Are you saying you want to use my urine to ice the runners on our sled?"

"That's right. Was there something else you wanted to save it for?"

"Of course not, but why do you need urine? Why can't we use any water for ice?"

"Fresh water ice is brittle. It will break too easily. Ice made from urine is tougher. It will last a lot longer."

"You are absolutely revolting. Do you seriously expect me to urinate on our sled runners?"

"No, we need to collect our urine, and let it cool until it is a little above freezing. Then we can pour it slowly on the runners."

"You're really serious, aren't you?"

"Of course. That is what the Eskimos did."

"Well, okay, but you had better not tell anyone about this if we ever make it back to civilization."

She didn't like his suggestion, but they really did need to find a way to make it easier to pull the sled. If his plan would enable them to reach another island before winter, it was worth a try.

The next morning they started out again with freshly iced sled runners. They pulled the sled a little way, and then they stopped to rest. It was a little easier, but progress was still slow. As they rested, he looked in every direction. She could tell he was thinking about something again.

"What is it this time, and I hope it is better than the last idea."

"I'm wondering what direction we should go."

"What? We are on the second day of our journey, and now you wonder what direction we should go? How about south?"

"We are going south. I just wonder if we should go straight south."

"Of course we should go straight south. What other direction do you think we should go?"

"I'm thinking about polar bears."

"Do you think there are more bears in one direction than in another?"

"We have no way of knowing."

"Then how can it make any difference which direction we go?"

"We want to go away from them."

"But you just said we don't know where they are."

"We don't know where they are, but they may know where we are."

"But if we don't know where they are, how can we go away from them?"

"That is simple. We can go upwind. That way we would be walking away from any bear that might smell us."

"So then, are you saying we should go west?"

"No, east."

"But the prevailing wind is from the west."

"No, the prevailing wind is from the east."

"Look, I have lived in Vancouver and Chicago. The prevailing wind is from the west."

"That is true. In the middle latitudes the prevailing wind is from the west, but in the Arctic the prevailing winds are the Polar Easterlies."

"Why is that?"

"It has to do with the heating of the air at the equator and the rotation of the earth."

"Okay, you don't have to give me all the details."

"I thought you didn't like short answers."

"I didn't say I don't like short answers; I just like complete sentences."

"Okay, but I think we should head southeast. That way we are still going in the right general direction, but we have the best chance of avoiding bears."

With that they took off again. By the time the sun set in the mid-afternoon, they had covered about five more miles. It was not a lot, but it was better than they had done the previous day. They could no longer see the island they had left. They also could not see anything else but ice.

Chapter 22 There's No House Like a Snow House

They set up their sealskin tent again. They had tried to go as fast as they could while they had sunlight. There would be plenty of time to eat and rest during the long night. In the morning they rose long before the sun came up in the mid forenoon. Days were rapidly getting shorter. Would they reach another island before the sun set for the winter? Surely with all the thousands of islands in the Arctic they would have to find one soon. If they didn't, they would have to spend the whole winter on the ice.

As soon as it was light enough, they took off again pulling their sled. They traveled as fast as they could because they knew they only had a few short hours of daylight. Another day passed, and they managed to cover another five miles. Progress seemed extremely slow. As they settled down to another long night, she asked him, "Isn't there some way we could go faster? We have been moving as fast as we can, and we haven't even gone fifteen miles yet."

"If we had dogs, we could probably go twenty-five miles per day. They typically run ten to fourteen miles per hour. Sometimes they run fifteen miles per hour with good conditions. During the Iditarod the teams typically cover 70 to 100 miles a day."

"They must have a lot more energy than I do."

"That is true. The dogs burn about 12,000 calories a day. That is the equivalent of 22 Big Macs."

"Wow! If I ate that much, I would look like the Goodyear blimp."

"You wouldn't if you ran a hundred miles a day."

"I'm not a dog."

"Just my luck."

"Oh, stop it. I know you would rather have a dog than me."

"Actually, I would need a whole team of dogs. One would not be enough."

"Well, whether you like dogs more than me or not, we don't have any."

"Observation would seem to confirm your analysis."

"What?"

"You're right."

"Why didn't you say that in the first place?"

"I thought you didn't like short answers."

"I just like complete sentences. Look, this whole conversation is pointless. We don't have dogs. Is there anything we can do to travel any faster?"

"The only thing I can think of is to abandon the sled, and we don't want to do that. We will just have to plod along as best we can."

With that they settled down for another long night. The next couple days they continued their slow progress. Then it began to snow. Visibility was too poor for them to proceed. They remained in their poor excuse for a tent for three days. They were running out of time, and they couldn't move until the storm ended. She was understandably discouraged.

"Why does everything have to go wrong? Our progress is pitifully slow, and now we can't travel at all because of the snow. I suppose you are going to tell me that somehow this storm is a really great thing."

"Right you are. As I told you last year, snow has many important uses. One thing we have been missing on our joyous romp across the ice is snow to build an igloo. Now we can enjoy all the pleasures of Eskimo life except a seal oil lamp.”

“Don't forget your wish that I was a dog.”

“I didn't say I wished you were a dog. I just wish we had dogs.”

“Well, just wave your magic wand, and turn me into a team of dogs.”

“That would be nice if I could, but I somehow forgot to pack my wand when we went on our little adventure.”

“Next time I hope you have more foresight.”

When the storm finally ended, they started off again. The snow made it even harder to pull the sled. The only consolation was that they were able to make an igloo each night. It definitely was an improvement over the crude tent they had been using. After a few more days they had to stop and assess their situation. There were only a couple of hours of sunlight each day, and that would end very soon. They estimated that they had traveled about forty miles, and there was no island in sight. Should they go on, or make an igloo to stay in for the rest of the winter? They had built an igloo around their sled, and as they sat in darkness inside they discussed their options.

“It is not likely that we can go more than another ten miles or so before the sun sets for the next three months. I am thinking that maybe we should leave the sled here and go a day's journey further to see if there is any sign of land.”

“I thought you said we couldn't abandon the sled.”

“We can't, but we can travel much faster without it. If I go ten or twenty miles and don't find anything, I can return.”

“I suppose that makes sense, but I'm not staying here alone.”

“I can travel faster without you.”

"There you go again. You always think you are better than me."

"Better than I"

"I don't care; I'm not staying here all by myself."

"I thought you didn't like being with me."

"I don't; but being alone is even worse."

"Okay, but you had better keep up."

"You are the one who will need to try to keep up."

The next morning they took enough food for a couple days and started their walk. They really wanted to find land. After the sun set, they continued until it was completely dark. They made a rough snow shelter and waited for daylight. When it was light enough to continue, they debated whether to head back to their sled or go a little further. Their eagerness won out over common sense. They decided to go on until the sun began to set. Then they made a little mound of snow, and while he stood on top of it, she stood on his shoulders and looked as far as she could see in every direction. There was nothing to see but ice. Disappointed, they headed back.

Since the northern lights were quite bright that night, they continued until they reached their shelter from the previous evening. They knew that meant that they would be able to get back to their sled the next day. After sleeping through the night, they awoke early. The sun would not rise for some time, but the sky was clear. Since it was light enough to see quite well, they thought about starting back, but they decided instead to build a more substantial igloo where they were. At first she didn't understand, but he explained his plan. They would make this their home for the winter. It was about ten miles further along than where they had left their sled. They couldn't reach another island before the sun set for the winter, but they could bring their sled to their winter home. That way they would be ten miles closer to their ultimate goal when they could begin traveling again.

In a couple hours they had a new igloo mostly completed. As the sun began to rise, they headed back to get their sled. A little after dark they arrived and spent the night there. It took three days to pull the sled to the place they had chosen to spend the winter. They were disappointed that they had not found any land or people, but they were better off than the previous winter. They had sufficient food and better clothes. Most importantly, they were fifty miles closer to home

So began their winter in their house of snow.

Chapter 23 Three More Months of Darkness

Naturally, she was very discouraged with the prospect of spending another cold winter in the dark with nothing to do. As usual, she began to complain.

"I don't want to stay with you inside this wretched pile of snow all winter. You promised we would be back in civilization by now."

"I made no such promise, and you know it."

"You said we might. That means it should be possible."

"Saying something is possible is not a guarantee."

"Well, I want to get back home now."

"So do I, but it is just not possible."

"We might as well have stayed back on the island. What happens when the ice melts in the spring?"

"We will have three months after the sun returns before the ice melts. It should take less than two months to walk all the way to the mainland."

"I suppose you are going to tell me again how lucky we are."

"We are better off than we were last year at this time. There is goose down in our sealskin clothes instead of mosses and lichens. Seal meat and fish are better than bear meat, and we have more of it. In fact, in some ways we have it even better than the Eskimos."

"As you like to point out, we don't have dogs. How are we better off than the Eskimos?"

"There are two big problems they had that we don't. Their big health concern was tuberculosis. It was introduced to them when they encountered Europeans. In the 1950s there were so many cases that the mortality rate was about 1 percent per year. Another problem they had was lice. That is a nuisance that is hard to get rid of. Lice can survive sub-zero temperatures. We have no one to give those problems to us."

"Gee, I didn't realize how lucky we are. Is there anything else they had a problem with that we don't have to worry about?"

"Well, there is alcohol. Some estimate that 95 percent of police calls among Eskimos are alcohol related. Most of the violence, murder and suicide is because of alcohol. That is why there are many places where it is banned or severely restricted. They still get it anyway."

"Okay, so we don't have tuberculosis, lice or alcohol. I still don't want to sit here in the dark until the sun rises on February 1st."

"January 29."

"What?"

"I said January 29th is when the sun is likely to rise for the first-time next year."

"But we already know it rises February 1st. Don't you remember from last winter?"

"We are about fifty miles further south. We gain another day with sunshine for each nine miles we go."

"How do you figure that?"

"It is simple. It is 1626 miles from the Arctic Circle to the North Pole. There is one day of no sun at the Arctic Circle and 183 days at the North Pole. Just do the math."

"No thanks. I'll take your word for it."

So it was that they settled down for another long wait for the sun to return. Again they celebrated Thanksgiving and Christmas as they had the previous year. Only this time they had more to be thankful for. Not only was there more and better meat, but they also had better clothes. It was still very cold, but they both had parkas and mukluks. That meant that they could both go outside at the same time. They walked every day that the weather allowed. It not only gave them exercise, but it also gave them something to do to reduce the boredom. This winter she didn't have the bouts of depression that she had had the previous year. She was becoming more "Eskimo".

November and December passed. As they got into January, she was feeling disgusted with the long wait for sunshine, but her anticipation of spring kept her going. She was experiencing disgust, not depression. It was not dangerous; it just had to be endured. By now they both had learned to endure.

As they got closer to the end of the month, they decided to play their guessing game again. He had estimated that the sun would rise January 29. She was skeptical, but since he was usually right, she didn't want to make a guess that was far off. She guessed January 30. It really didn't matter who was closer, but the anticipation made life less boring.

They were finally into the last week of January. They were interested to see who would win their little game. She was eager to continue their journey.

"Actually, I hope you win this time. I can't wait to get going. I've put up with your stench for as long as I can stand it. Do you think we can leave as soon as the sun rises?"

"I don't think that would be wise. Remember that February is the coldest month in the Arctic. Also, we want to wait until there are more hours of daylight. I think we should wait until March to start out again. It won't be quite so bitterly cold, and we still will have three months before the spring melt. That should be enough to find another island or reach the mainland."

"Another delay? We've already waited all winter."

"It is better to wait and make it home than to be in too big of a rush and end up dead."

"Yes, but they say the early bird gets the worm."

"That is true, but it is also true that the second mouse gets the cheese."

"The second mouse? Oh, I get it. The first mouse gets caught in the trap. Very funny."

"It's not funny for the first mouse. We need to use our heads if we want to stay alive."

"Okay, you win; we can wait until March. At least, it will be nice to see the sun again."

This time his guess was right. The sun rose on January 29. Spring was near.

Chapter 24 On the Move Again

The thrill of seeing the sun again made it easier to accept another month's delay in continuing their journey, but both were eager to get started. They had enough to eat, and their sealskin clothes made the sub-zero temperatures bearable. Again the days rapidly got longer after the sun finally rose above the horizon. This time it would be easier to pull the sled because they had eaten over half the meat that they had when they started their journey.

On the first of March the temperature was still thirty below zero, but they were so eager to get started that they decided to leave anyway. They could always build another snow igloo if they needed to. It would be no different than the home they had lived in all winter. Maybe in a few days they would find another island.

The first day they covered about five miles. They had more hours of sunlight, but they were tired and decided to stop and build an igloo. They had been doing some walking through the winter, but pulling the sled made them more tired than they had expected. There was no big rush since they had three months before the ice would melt.

The next few days they continued to progress five to ten miles a day. They were heading in a south-easterly direction. As he had pointed out, they wanted to travel upwind so that they would be moving away from any bear that might smell them. Each day they stopped a couple hours before dark to build another igloo.

Everything was going well until the second week of March. His main concern all along had been bears. Periodically he would get on top of the sled and look as far as he could see in every direction. If there were any bears, he wanted to see them while they were a long way off.

One day as he searched the horizon, he thought he saw something. Everything was white except the blue sky, but he thought he saw something that looked different than the rest of the ice and snow. As he continued to watch, he noticed that it was moving. He continued to watch a few more minutes. It was northwest of them and was headed in their direction. It was following their trail. He told her, and she immediately became terrified.

"Oh no! What can we do?"

"For now let's go as fast as we can in the same direction we are headed."

"Won't it follow us?"

"It probably will, but it will likely go three and a half miles per hour. If we can go faster than that, we can get further away from it. Maybe it will smell a seal and stop following our tracks."

"Do you think that is likely?"

"No."

"Then what good will it do to keep going?"

"Do you want to stay here and wait for it?"

"No."

"Then let's go."

"Okay, but it will eventually catch up to us. You are always showing off how smart you are. Think of something."

"I will think while we are walking."

They pulled their sled as fast as they could for another hour. Then he got on top of it again and looked to see if the bear was still following them. It was, and it was a little closer. It was obvious that it could smell them, and it was following their tracks. What could they do? He tried to think. Sight and smell;

that was the problem. How could they keep the bear from smelling them and seeing their tracks? They could circle around so that they were downwind, but the bear would still follow their tracks. How could they keep the bear from seeing the tracks? Then he had an idea. The bear was still a long way off. It was looking at the tracks but not at them. They could travel in a big circle. Then when they were downwind, they could jump off the trail and cover their tracks. Hopefully, the bear would continue to follow around in a circle until it realized that they were no longer on that trail. By then they would be downwind, and it would not know where to look for them.

They had a plan. It might not work, but it was worth a try. The alternative was to keep going as they were until the bear caught up with them and killed them. They set off, moving as quickly as they could. The circle had to be big enough so that the bear would not realize it was going in a circle. At the same time, they had to complete the circle before the bear got close enough to easily see them. They counted on the fact that the bear would be looking down at the tracks and not scanning the horizon to see them.

They continued on until they got back to their previous tracks. Then they followed them, trying to step in the exact same footsteps as before. When they were downwind, they both got on top of the sled. Then he threw her as far as he could off the trail. She made sure she landed on her feet. He then proceeded to throw the meat to her one piece at a time. After everything was off the sled, he pulled it another hundred feet or so along the trail. Then he picked it up and threw it away from their tracks. He walked further, and then retraced his steps walking backward in the same footsteps. Hopefully, the bear would not realize they had left the trail until they were far away. Making the longest standing broad jump he could, he left the trail. He recovered the sled, brought it to where she was waiting, reloaded the meat and started pulling it toward the west. She followed behind to brush out their tracks.

After going a few hundred feet, they figured that the bear probably would not find their trail again. She stopped hiding the tracks and helped pull the sled. They proceeded as fast as they could for another mile. Then they stopped to rest and check on the bear. He was just visible in the distance, and their ruse seemed to be working. He was going around in a big circle.

After a rest they decided it was time to go again. What direction should they go? They had to stay downwind from the bear, and they wanted to go south. Southwest seemed to be the best choice. When they thought they were far enough away that the bear would not bother them again, they would head south east again. That way they would be moving away from any other bear that might catch their scent. She wondered how likely it was that they would encounter another bear.

"How many bears are there in the Arctic?"

"It is difficult to get an exact number because they are spread out over a very large area, and it is difficult to count them because there are very few observers. However, it is estimated that there are 22,000 to 31,000."

"I wish there were none."

"At the moment I would agree, but not everyone feels that way. There are laws protecting polar bears in all five nations that have them."

"What five nations?"

"Canada, United States, Greenland, Norway and Russia. In fact, during the Cold War about the only thing the US and the USSR agreed on was restrictions on polar bear hunting."

"Do you mean that no one can hunt polar bears anymore?"

"No, some countries don't allow any hunting, but others set limits to how many can be taken each year. In Canada about

600 bears are killed each year. Around 80 percent of those are from Nunavut, where we are."

"I don't see why anybody would want to protect an animal as dangerous as a polar bear."

"I understand, but there are arguments for their preservation."

"But they kill people."

"That is true, but people kill a lot more of them. There have only been two or three people killed by polar bears in the last ten years. They live in very sparsely populated areas, and most people who encounter them either have guns or they have vehicles to get away."

"I don't see why they would be here since there is nothing for them to eat."

"A bear can go eight months without eating."

"You're kidding. You must be talking about when they hibernate."

"They don't hibernate."

"Everyone knows bears hibernate."

"Other bears do, but polar bears do not. The closest thing to hibernation among polar bears is the time the females enter the maternity dens in the fall. They don't sleep much, but their heart rate slows from 46 to 27 beats per minute. Their body temperature does not drop like animals that hibernate."

"I don't see how they can go eight months without eating if they don't hibernate."

"The mother bears double their weight before fall when they enter their dens."

"They must have really big babies."

"No, the cubs are only a couple pounds when they are born."

"Why do they gain so much weight if the babies are so small?"

"They have to nurse the cubs from mid-winter until spring without eating anything, and they normally have two of them."

"So then, are you saying they nurse their young for about three months?"

"No, it is usually two and a half years."

"I thought you said they nurse them until spring."

"Spring is when they come out of their dens to hunt seals. Wouldn't you be hungry after eight months?"

"I'd be dead. Wait a minute. It's March. Are the bears leaving their dens about now?"

"That's right."

"Do you think we will get to see some bear cubs?"

"You had better hope not. Like all bears, polar bears are very protective of their young. A mother bear would kill you just as a safety precaution."

With that they concluded their discussion. They continued to travel as fast as they could until a little before dark. Since they could see no sign of the bear, they decided that it was safe to stop for the night and build an igloo. They rested uneasily until morning.

Chapter 25 More Bears

Rising long before daylight, he looked around cautiously. There was no sign of any bear. They wanted to get started again. Wanting to be sure the bear didn't have a chance to catch their scent, they continued heading southwest. They traveled as fast as they could all day because they wanted to put as much distance between them and the bear as they could. As usual they built an igloo at the end of the day.

The next morning when they started out they decided that they had lost the bear, and it was time to turn southeast again. Progress was good for a couple days. Surely they would find another island soon.

On the third day it began to snow. Visibility was poor, but they wanted to keep going. Surely the storm would slow a bear as much as it did them. They were wrong.

About midday they looked behind them and saw that a bear was just a few hundred feet away. She screamed. He normally would have told her to keep quiet, but it didn't matter. The bear could easily see them anyway. Their previous trick of going in a big circle would not work either. What could they do? He had to think fast. Then he remembered his plan while they were still back on the island. The bear was hungry. They could leave a seal for it to eat. Hopefully, they could escape while it ate.

"Let's run," she said with terror in her voice.

"No, if we run the bear will chase us. We can't outrun a polar bear."

"We can't just keep walking until it catches up with us."

"That is just what I am counting on."

"Are you insane?"

"I have a plan. Keep pulling on the sled while I retrieve the pup."

"What are you going to do?"

"I will put the seal inside my clothes to warm it up."

"What possible good will that do?"

"I am hoping that a bear would prefer a thawed seal to a frozen one."

"What do you mean?"

"I plan to offer the pup to the bear so that it will eat it, and we can escape."

"Not my baby!"

"It's not your baby. It is an animal. Would you prefer that the bear eat you?"

"Of course not, but are you sure it will work?"

"I am not at all sure, but my guess is that the bear is hungry and just wants something to eat. Let's give it a try. I can't think of anything else."

"Okay, but I hope the bear doesn't get any closer."

"I hope it will. I want it to see the seal when I throw it."

"Ooooooh! I am so scared."

"So am I, but we need to keep our wits about us."

With that he untied the rope holding his parka together and slipped the pup inside. Needless to say, it was very cold. Retying the rope, he grabbed the sled rope and helped her pull. They continued walking briskly, but they didn't run. Every few minutes they looked back to see how far behind the bear was. He knew that the normal hunting practice of polar bears is to creep up slowly on a seal and then suddenly rush to make the kill. Timing was important. He wanted to throw the seal to the bear just before it was ready to make its charge. His guess was that fifty feet would be the distance in question.

They were walking as fast as they could, but the bear was slowly gaining on them. It was a hundred and fifty feet away. Then it was a hundred feet. If his guess was wrong, they would be dead before he had a chance to put his plan into effect. When the bear was a little over fifty feet behind them, he had her keep pulling the sled while he took the pup out of his parka. Holding it firmly, he tossed it about twenty feet toward the bear.

This was not something the bear had expected. It stopped and stood on its hind legs to observe. What had the man thrown onto the trail? Dropping back down, it walked to the object lying on the ice. It was a small seal, which was the bear's preferred food. It had been looking for something to eat, and here was a meal that it could have without any effort. It stopped to eat while the people continued to walk on. It didn't need to worry about them getting away since it could easily follow their scent.

They kept walking until the snow obscured their view of the bear. Then they turned to the right in a big arc. If they could get downwind before the bear resumed following them, maybe they could get away. As soon as they thought the bear could no longer see them, they started to run. It was hard to pull the sled while running, but they had to put as much distance between them and the bear as they could. After going a half mile or so, they were exhausted. Again he threw her off the trail, tossed the meat to her, and then pulled the sled a little further. After going on a bit, he threw the sled, walked a little more, backtracked stepping in the same footprints, and then jumped off the trail himself. It had worked before; hopefully it would work again. One advantage they had was that it was snowing. Their tracks should soon be covered.

When they had recovered the sled and the meat, they headed west. They moved swiftly and quietly. After going a mile or so, she thought the bear probably could not hear them.

"Do you think the bear will follow us?"

"I'm sure it will try."

"But we gave it food. Won't it be satisfied?"

"If you feed a stray dog, it will always come back for more. The bear got food by following us. I'm sure it will try to follow us again."

"Then your idea was really dumb."

"Did you have a better idea?"

"You are the one who is supposed to know everything."

"I never said I know everything. Giving the bear the pup was all I could think of."

"Well, I hope you have a better idea next time."

"If I didn't have this idea, there wouldn't be a next time."

"Well, okay, but I've never been so scared in my life."

"What about the time we encountered the bear back on the island?"

"That time I was past being scared; I thought there was no hope at all."

"So, was this experience better or worse?"

"I don't know, but I hope we never get this close to a bear again."

"You have a point. From now on let's not travel unless there is clear visibility."

With that they stopped talking and concentrated on getting as far from the bear as they could. Just in case it did succeed in following them, they zigzagged back and forth. Each time they changed directions, they brushed out their tracks. The snow would make their footprints hard to follow, but they wanted to make it as difficult as possible. Even if they got away from this bear, there might be others.

A couple hours before dark they changed directions again. This time they headed straight south. Normally they would have stopped to build an igloo, but their fear kept them going. When they were too weary to go on, they stopped and made a very crude snow shelter.

In the morning the snow had stopped, and the visibility was good again. There didn't seem to be any sign of the bear. Just to be sure, he got on top of the sled and had her stand on his shoulders to look around. The snow had covered their tracks, and she couldn't see any sign of danger. They both breathed a sigh of relief.

Since the coast was clear, they both wanted to make the most of the good weather while it lasted. They continued south for a half a day. Then they resumed their normal southeasterly direction. The next few days were uneventful, for which they were thankful. They made good progress.

By the last week of March they had covered about another hundred miles from their winter camp. Everything seemed to be going well until one morning when he woke up a little earlier than normal. Had something disturbed his sleep? He listened carefully. Was something outside? He wondered if he should awake her. If she woke up unexpectedly, she might make a noise that would cause more trouble. He decided it would be best to wake her up and warn her to be very quiet. Putting his hand over her mouth, he shook her. When she awoke, he whispered in her ear, "I thought I heard something outside. I'm going to open the entrance and take a look."

She whispered back, "Be careful."

Of course that went without saying. He was tempted to point out that fact but doing so would be as worthless as what she had said, and they had much more important things to deal with.

He took his spear and crept toward the entrance. She was a little behind him. As soon as he opened the entrance, he saw a bear's head just a couple feet in front of him. She screamed in terror. The bear was almost as startled as they were. The scream hurt its ears, and it retreated a few feet. A bear has nothing to fear, but it didn't like that shrill noise. In its world there is little sound. It had killed many seals, but it had never encountered anything so offensive before.

The man noticed the bear's reaction. There would be no chance to get away this time. They were in the igloo, and the bear was outside. What could they do? It could easily tear apart their flimsy house of snow. Was this the end?

The bear stood there for a few minutes. There was food inside that bunch of snow. This was a little different from grabbing a seal from a breathing hole and pulling it up onto the ice. It had not encountered such strange creatures before, and they made an awful sound. Still they were food, and it was hungry. This matter needed more investigation. It approached the hole in the snowbank again.

The man saw the bear coming and readied his spear. How could he dissuade it from getting too close? If he stabbed it, that would probably anger it but not kill it. Maybe he could just make it uncomfortable enough to get it to back off. As the bear stuck its head into the entrance, he poked its nose. At the same time she screamed in terror again. The bear withdrew again.

These strange creatures were different from any it had ever dealt with. Why couldn't they just let it grab them and start eating? Why did they have to hurt its nose and make that awful racket? This was annoying. It was just hungry and wanted to eat.

He noticed again the bear's reaction. He pointed it out to her and recommended that she try to scream as loud and shrill as she could every time the bear approached. At the same time he would be ready with his spear.

The bear tried a couple more times with the same results. Then it lay down on the ice to think and wait. Maybe the creatures would come out after a while, and it could have a meal. Seals had to come out of their holes every twenty minutes or so.

The waiting game began. After a couple hours the bear tried again. The results were still the same. It was a standoff. The bear would not go away, and they didn't dare come out of the igloo. The whole day passed. Night was coming on. They didn't dare go to sleep. Would the bear try to kill them while it was dark? They had to remain vigilant.

By morning they were very tired, but they didn't dare fall asleep. The bear tried a few more times to approach them, but it always got a poke in the nose and had to endure that awful sound. This was not working out well at all. It just wanted something to eat, and it wasn't getting anything. Maybe there was an easier way to get food. It really wanted seals anyway.

When the third day arrived, they didn't see the bear. Maybe it was behind the igloo waiting to attack them as soon as they came out. That was a chance they didn't want to take. When there was no sign of the bear for a couple hours, they decided to take turns sleeping. The day passed with no sign of the bear.

The next morning he cautiously looked outside. There was no danger that he could see from the entrance. He listened intently. Ever so slowly he inched his way out. He knew that a seal often doesn't see a bear until it grabs it, and then it is too late.

As soon as his head was out enough to see around the igloo, he stepped outside and looked over the surroundings. There was no sign of the bear. Then he went over to where the bear had been and looked at its tracks. It had headed east. Maybe it had picked up the scent of a seal.

That was it. They quickly recovered their sled and headed southwest again. Surely there had to be an island out there somewhere. They had to find someplace that they would be safe from bears.

Chapter 26 Land

They traveled all day, and then made an igloo as they normally did. In the morning they headed southeast again. This zigzagging back and forth meant that they were not progressing south as fast as they would have been otherwise. However, avoiding bears was their main concern. There was still plenty of time to reach the mainland before the spring thaw.

He couldn't understand why they had not found another island yet. With over 36,000 islands and three of the ten largest islands in the world in the Canadian Arctic they should have found one by now. Not only that, but the Canadian islands are right next to Greenland, which is the largest island in the world. How could their luck be so bad?

They kept plodding along. By now it was the middle of April. At least temperatures were in the teens again, and they could travel until they were exhausted because there were over fourteen hours of sunlight every day. In another month they could go all day if they had the strength because the sun would shine twenty-four hours a day. Even with all the delays and the changes of direction, he estimated that they were about two hundred miles south of their starting point.

They kept scanning the horizon for any sign of land or danger. That was probably why they were paying little attention to the ice they were walking on. As they trudged along, he suddenly disappeared from beside her. There was a splashing sound, and she squealed with surprise and fright. Then she realized what had happened. He had fallen into a hole in the ice. He was still clutching the sled rope. She quickly grabbed the rope, and he pulled himself out of the hole.

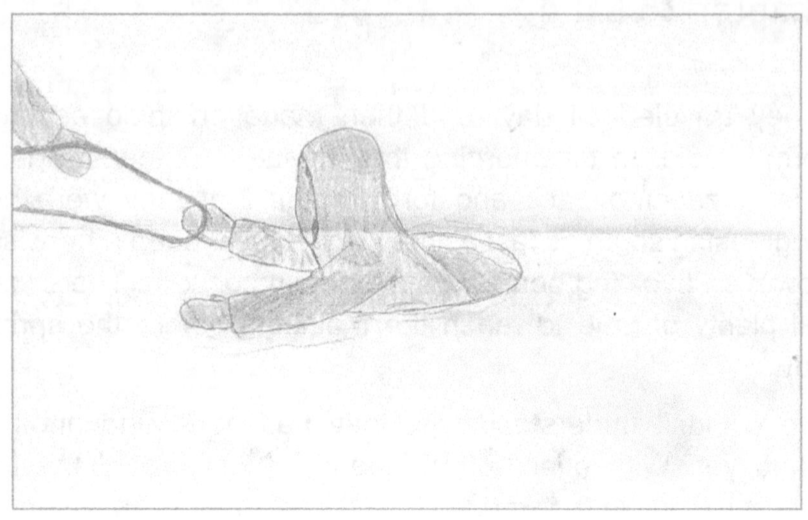

Figure 9 Falling Through the Ice

At once he understood the danger he was in. Eskimos try to avoid sweating because in sub-zero temperatures, any moisture can quickly freeze and endanger their lives. He quickly brushed the water from his face and beard. Fortunately her excellent sewing had made his clothes almost waterproof. A little water had gotten down his neck. It was really cold at first, but his body heat soon warmed it. Fortunately, it was a warm day. The temperature was nearly twenty degrees. He grabbed a seal skin they had used for a tent and a blanket and put it over his head. His breath warmed the interior of the covering, which in turned warmed his face.

"What are you doing?" she asked.

His voice was a little muffled through the seal skin. "I am trying to keep my face from freezing."

"I see. Are you okay? You gave me quite a scare."

"I will be okay. I just need a couple minutes to warm up my face."

"For a smart guy, you are really dumb sometimes. Why weren't you watching where you were going?" She was really relieved that he was okay, but she couldn't bring herself to say so.

"So then, are you admitting that you think I am smart?"

"I was pointing out how dumb it was to fall into that hole. Wait. Why was there a hole in the ice?"

He pulled the seal skin off his face. "I can only think of one possibility. It must be a seal breathing hole. This is the first one we have found."

"Does that mean there are seals near here?"

"If there were not, the hole would have frozen over a long time ago."

"I didn't think their breathing holes would be so big."

"The size of their holes varies, but a couple feet in diameter is common."

"If there are seals here, that means we might be able to catch one."

"That is true. It is also true that a bear might catch one."

"Oh no, let's get out of here."

"I agree. I think I am ready to go on now."

They moved as fast as they could the rest of the day. Now they were not only watching the horizon, but they were also watching for holes in the ice. Fortunately, the water evaporated, and he suffered no long-term harm.

A couple days later, as they were pulling the sled, he thought he saw something in the distance. At first he thought it was a low-lying cloud, but it didn't seem to ever move. It was to the southwest of them. They were heading southeast as they usually did. Since the apparent cloud didn't ever move, they decided to investigate. They turned toward it and continued for a couple hours. It still didn't move, and it was getting bigger. Could it be what they had been looking for all these months? After so many disappointments, they didn't want to get their hopes up, but as they got closer, it certainly did look like   LAND.

She asked, "Do you really think it could be?"

"It could. Stand on my shoulders and see if you can get a better look."

She did, and then he asked, "Well, how about it? Does it look like land?"

"I think so. Let me down, and let's run to it."

"Don't get too excited. If it is land, it won't go anywhere. It has to be a good ten miles away."

He let her down. She was anxious to go. "Come on, I want to see if it really is land."

"Whoa. Easy girl, easy."

"Will you stop that? I'm not a horse."

"I know. You're a blond."

"There you go again. How many times to I have to tell you…"?

"Settle down. I told you I like blonds."

"But I want to see if it really is land."

"Like I said, if it is land, it will still be land in the morning."

"In the morning! I don't want to wait that long."

"I've told you before that if we want to survive and get back home, we need to use our heads."

"What's that got to do with anything? We have been looking for land, and now it seems like we have found it."

"It is nearly dark. There could be a bear waiting there to kill us. We can't get there before nightfall. Let's build an igloo and start out in the morning."

That stopped her in her tracks. She had temporarily forgotten about bears. Again she remembered the terror she had experienced several times over the last few months. If there were bears, she certainly didn't want to encounter them. Why did he always have to be right?

"Okay, I guess I can handle one more night on the ice. Let's get to work on the igloo."

In the morning they rose early even though they had only had about five hours of sleep. They both wanted to see the island if that was what it was. As soon as it was light, she got on his shoulders again. It looked the same as it had the evening before. Surely a cloud would have moved by now. He instructed her to look carefully in every direction for bears. When they were satisfied that there were none, they quickly broke camp and headed toward their island. Maybe there would be people there. They could be home soon.

They were excited, and the sled was easier to pull now that they had less than a hundred pounds of meat left. They thought about carrying the meat and leaving the sled, but they had learned not to abandon anything unless they had to. As the day progressed, the island got bigger and bigger. By midday there was no longer any question of whether or not it was land. The only question was what land it might be. It certainly could not be the mainland since that had to be about three hundred miles away yet. Maybe it was Somerset or Prince of Wales Island. He didn't think it could be Victoria Island since that was probably farther south. It was big, but maybe it wasn't one of the bigger islands.

Even with their brisk pace, it seemed like it was taking forever to reach the island. It was fortunate that the sun didn't set until after nine o'clock. About twilight they reached the shore. The last half mile had taken much longer because the tides had caused the ice to break up nearer the land. They had to be very careful where they walked. That was okay. They had reached land.

Chapter 27 Arctic Paradise

Since twilight lasted a couple hours after sunset, they had plenty of time to build an igloo before it became too dark to work. They settled down to sleep, but they were too excited to rest very long. Twilight returned before 3 in the morning. Before the sun rose they got up and ate breakfast. Maybe there would be people on the island. They could be back home in a couple days. She naturally wanted to know where they were.

"What island do you think we are on?"

"It is impossible to know our longitude, but I think our latitude is about that of Prince of Wales Island."

"Do you think that is where we are?"

"We don't know yet. If it is, it's the tenth largest island in Canada."

"That must mean there are a lot of people here."

"There are no people on Prince of Wales Island.'

"I thought you said it is the tenth largest island in Canada. If there are people at Resolute, and we are two hundred miles south of there, there should be people here."

"Maybe there should be, but there are not."

''Are there any other islands nearby that have people?"

"Not anymore."

"What do you mean?"

"Somerset Island is just east of Prince of Wales Island. There were people there at one time."

"When?"

"A thousand years ago."

"That's a long time. How do you even know they were there?"

"Explorers have found whale bones, tunnels and stone ruins. From 1937 to 1948 the Hudson Bay Company had a trading post there, but it has been uninhabited since the post closed."

"I guess that means it wouldn't do us much good if it were Somerset."

"Actually, that would be good because Somerset Island is separated from the Boothia Peninsula by the Bellot Strait. It is just over a mile wide."

"Why should we care about that?"

"The Boothia Peninsula is the northernmost point of the Canadian mainland. If we could get there, we could just walk along the coast until we found a native village."

"Do you think we could be on Somerset Island?"

"I don't think so, but we need to start exploring."

"Okay, I'm eager to get home. How do we proceed?"

"I think the thing to do is to go inland first to a high hill and see what we can find."

"Fine. Let's do it."

With that they headed to the highest point they could see. Since they intended to return to their igloo, they left the sled and took enough meat to last a couple days. When they reached the high point, they could see another that was even higher. They went on to that. It took a couple hours, and when they got there, they looked around. They could see the ocean to the south, but all they could see to the west and north was more land. It was a large island, but they couldn't tell how large. There were hills and valleys in every direction. After resting a bit they retraced their steps.

When they got back to their shelter on the shore, they sat down to consider their next move. She asked, "What do you think we should do now?"

Well, what we need is information. We need to know if this really is an island or if it is part of the mainland. If it is an island, we want to know how big it is. Most of all we want to know if there are any inhabitants."

"I hope so. I want to get home. What's the next step?"

"I suggest we take the sled and go along the shore to the south. That is the general direction we want to go anyway. If this is an island as we think it is, we will eventually get back to our starting point. Then we will know how big it is, and we will have more knowledge of the area."

She thought for a minute. "That sounds reasonable, but why should we take the sled if we are coming back here anyway? Couldn't we travel faster without it?"

"We could, but we don't know what we will find. If we don't get back here, we want everything with us."

"Okay, let's get started."

"No, I think we should wait until tomorrow. It is afternoon now. Let's rest and start early in the morning."

She was impatient, but after a year and a half she had learned to trust his judgment. With all the walking they had done and the short rest the previous night, some extra sleep would be nice. They didn't even have to build an igloo since they could use the one from the day before. That was a nice change.

The next morning they rose early to start their exploration. By midday the shoreline turned to the west. Later in the afternoon they came across a small stream that emptied into the ocean. In most places it was frozen over, but where the descent was steeper, it was not. Here was a chance to get a drink without having to thaw snow.

He remarked, "Things just keep getting better and better for us. We have food and clothing. Now we have a much larger estate. We even have running water for the first time."

"We still don't have fire. Just give me fire, and maybe I will agree with you."

"I have every confidence in your ability to complain even if we do get fire." He thought for a minute and then continued, "Fire would be nice. Maybe, sometime, we will get that too, but for now we need to continue learning what we can about our surroundings. Let's follow the stream up the hill."

They did so, and after they came to the source, they continued to the top of the hill. It was a few hundred feet above the sea. They stopped to rest and look around. There were hills and valleys all around. From their vantage point they had a great view of the bay below. It was really quite majestic. After resting a bit they returned to the sled on the shore. They continued along the coast until late in the evening. By then the shoreline was turning toward the north. They stopped for the night.

In the morning they continued. Around noon they saw a rather high hill and decided to go to the top and see what was visible. The view was about the same as they had seen from other hills. There was nothing but ocean to the west, and they couldn't see anything but more of the island to the north and east. Returning to the sled, they continued along the shore until evening. The next day they continued to follow the coast as it turned east. Late in the day it turned south again. It was now clear that they were on an island. The sun set, but they decided to continue in the twilight until they got back to their igloo. It was midnight when they reached it, but it was still light enough to see where they were going.

Being tired from their long walk, they slept later than normal in the morning. Then they ate and considered their next move.

She spoke first, "Well, now we know we are on an island, and we know it is a rather big one. It is obvious that there are no people here. What do we do now?"

"I think we know enough about the island for now. What we don't know is if there are any other islands near us. We want to go south. If there is another island south of us, we want to know about it."

"So, what do you suggest?"

"Do you remember that stream?"

"Of course, what about it?"

"It is mid-forenoon. The stream is on the south side of the island. We could go there and stop for the night. Tomorrow we could head south across the ice. We need to know if there is any other land within walking distance of our island. If not, we can then try west and north."

"What about east?"

"We came from the east."

"Oh, yeah. Don't you dare say anything about my hair color."

"It never crossed my mind."

"Yeah, right. I know what you are thinking."

The plan was simple enough. By evening they had reached the stream. When they were there before, they had continued on until late in the evening. That meant that they didn't have an igloo to stay in. That was not a problem. They had become quite expert at building igloos. Besides, their plan was to go south a day's journey and then return if they found nothing. They could reuse the same igloo when they returned. It was nice not to have to build a new house every day.

The next day they started out as soon as they could. If there was another island, they needed to know. The sled was left at the igloo by the stream. Whether they found another island or not, they would return, and they could travel faster without a sled to pull. After being encumbered with the sled all winter, walking without it seemed easy. They walked as fast as they could all day, and by evening they had covered over thirty miles. As the sun was setting around 10 o'clock, she got onto his shoulders and looked as far as she could see in every direction. There was nothing. They were a little disappointed, but at least they had learned more about their surroundings. It was light enough all night to travel because of the twilight, but they were tired after moving as fast as they could all day. With temperatures in the upper teens they decided to roll up in their sealskin blankets to sleep for a few hours rather than take time to build another snow shelter.

It was colder than they liked, and after getting some rest, they decided it was time to head back to the island. They walked slower than they had the day before. It was partly because they were tired and partly because they were disappointed that there was no island that they could find.

As they walked, they were careful to observe the condition of the ice. Several times they found spots that looked different than the rest of the ice. Upon investigating they discovered that there were seal breathing holes. Since he had fallen into one before, they were more alert now. A couple times they even saw seals come up for a breath of air. Their supply of meat was getting low. It was good to know that there were seals around. They didn't have time to hunt now, but soon they would need to take time to replenish their supplies.

The sun set before they got back to the island, but with the twilight they continued until they were able to return to their igloo. The next day they continued their plan of exploration. They reached the igloo they had made on the west end of the island. Their intention was to go a day's walk west, but then a snowstorm arose. It continued for three days. There was nothing to do but wait until it ended. When it finally did, they explored to the west, found nothing and returned to the island. Again they proceeded to the north of the island, explored, found nothing and returned.

As they sat in the igloo on the north shore of the island, they considered their next move.

"We've looked all around, and it is apparent that we are far from any other island. Now we have to decide if we should stay here or head south in hopes of finding another island or the mainland before the ice begins to melt."

"How long will that be?" she wanted to know.

"It is near the end of April. In May the temperatures will rise above the freezing point. We might make it to the mainland before the spring thaw, or we might find another island. If we have delays like we have had before, we could be in the middle of the Arctic Ocean when the ice breaks up. We could find ourselves on an ice floe drifting around until it all melts."

That didn't sound very good. She wanted to get back home but drowning in the Arctic Ocean was terrifying. Not knowing what to do, she asked, "What do you suggest?"

"We have stayed alive until now by being cautious. It is uncertain whether we can reach land before the thaw. I think the smart thing to do is to stay here."

"But I want to get back home. Are you suggesting that we stay here another whole year?"

"Yes, that is the logical course of action."

"I don't care about logic. I just want to go home."

"I do too. What do you suggest?"

"I don't know. You are supposed to be so smart; think of something."

"What I think is that we are much better off than we were up until now. We have adequate clothes. We know there are seals, which means there are fish. The birds will soon return. There is a good chance we will have caribou here. There is a nice stream on the south side of the island. We can build a better house. I think we can even make a fire this summer."

"I suppose next you are going to tell me this place is a veritable paradise."

Chapter 28 A New Home

That settled it. They would stay until the next winter. She didn't like the idea, but as disappointed as she was, she knew that was the only sensible thing to do. They would just have to make the best of it.

One thing they were in complete agreement on was that they would make their new home near the stream on the south side of the island. Since they now knew they had plenty of time, they didn't rush. The next day they made their way to the igloo they had made on the east side of the island, and the following day they returned to the one on the south side. She wanted to just rest there for a while, but he reminded her that the temperatures would soon be rising above freezing.

"Why is that a problem? I am tired of being cold all the time."

"We live in a snow house. It will melt."

She thought back to the previous spring. He had removed the snow from their stone shelter before it all turned to water. Now their house was made of all snow.

"What did the Eskimos do when their igloos melted?"

"They normally only stayed in snow igloos when they were on a journey. Usually they had sod or stone shelters for more permanent dwellings. In the summer they normally stayed in sealskin tents. If they were staying in a snow igloo when spring came, the children often played on the top of it until it caved in. The parents didn't punish them for doing that because that told them that it was warming up and it was time to move off the ice and onto the land."

"If I had a child and he caved in my house, I would punish him."

"The Eskimos were very lenient with their children. It was difficult to raise a child to adulthood because of all the dangers and frequent lack of food. If a child misbehaved, the adults said that they were glad to see it."

"That doesn't make sense. Why would they be glad to see a child misbehave?"

"They said they were glad to see it because they knew that the children would become more mature as they got older. It would be worse if people became less mature as they got older."

"I still say that doesn't make sense."

"If you had a child, and you didn't know if he would be alive in another year, wouldn't you be considerate of him?"

"I suppose so."

"Well, since we will have to stay here until next winter, we need to start house shopping. Would you prefer ranch or colonial?"

"You are not funny. I didn't notice any real estate office anywhere on our new island."

"Really? Let's go on up the hill and look around. Maybe we just missed it last time."

"You know very well there is nobody here but us."

"If that is true, then we get to be our own real estate agents. I think we can get a great bargain on an undeveloped building site."

"I hope you can recommend a good construction company."

"I can. It is the Him and Her Luxury Estates Home Builders. They have already built every home in this entire vast domain."

"Might I remind you that they were all one room dwellings, and they were made of snow with an expected useful life of about a month?"

"Yes but remember that not one failed to pass a housing inspection."

"Will you get serious?"

"Okay, so tell me about your dream home."

"Do you mean I don't have to settle for another little one room pile of rocks like we had on the other island?"

"Of course not. Now that we are filthy rich real estate tycoons, we can have anything we want. We can even have two rooms. In fact, if you want to be really extravagant, the day could come when we even add a third."

"What possible use could we find for a third room?"

"I'm thinking that a pantry might be nice."

"It would be nice if I didn't have to put up with your stench all the time, and another thing, I hate it when you snore."

"I don't snore."

"Yes, you do."

"I never heard myself snore."

"That's because you are asleep."

"Well okay, but let's go up the hill and see where we want to build our mansion."

With that they again followed the stream to its source. Then they continued to the top of the nearest hill. As before, they were impressed with the magnificent view. She looked around and thought to herself that maybe it would not be so awfully bad to stay here another year. One thing that was certain was that they would want to live near the stream so that they could always have fresh running water. It seemed like a great luxury after the difficulty they had had in obtaining adequate drinking water for the last year and a half.

A short distance down from the spring there was a fairly level spot where the stream made a little pool. That seemed like just the place to build their new home. Fortunately they agreed.

He remarked, "It is lucky for us that we got here before the big land rush. We get to have the pick of the best properties."

"I don't think we need to be too concerned about being crowded out very soon."

"Maybe not immediately, but just think how the value of our real estate investment will skyrocket when all the other eager home buyers start pouring in."

As she thought about how ludicrous his statement was, she finally could no longer suppress a laugh. "Okay, Mr. Know-It-All, I can see that we are not only the luckiest people in the world, but I have the good fortune to be partners with the most astute businessman of all time."

"That is very perceptive of you."

"Oh, stop it. You don't want your head to explode. It is swelling up more every minute."

"Hey, I am willing to share the glory with you. We both agreed on the wisdom of acquiring prime waterfront property."

"I just wanted to be able to get a drink more easily."

"Ah, my little cerebral flat line, you were wiser than you knew."

"I've had enough of your insults." She tried to be angry with him, but the whole thing seemed so funny that she couldn't help laughing.

After they both had a good laugh, it was time to settle down to work. "Okay," she said. "We know where we will build, but what do we use for building material?"

"As I have pointed out before, the options are snow, wood, sod, stone and animal hides. We don't have wood, snow will melt, and animal hides are for temporary summer dwellings. That leaves sod and stone. On the other island stone was our only choice. Do you see how our options have doubled?"

"So many choices make my head spin. You know how it is with blonds." Now she was insulting herself. They both had to laugh again.

"Okay," he said. "Variety is the spice of life. Let's try sod this time. Besides, it is easier to form into whatever shape we want."

"That's fine, but in case you haven't noticed, the sod is all frozen solid."

"It won't be much longer. It is almost the first of May. Temperatures will be rising above the thawing point in just a few more days."

"I hope so; I'm fed up with the cold."

They examined the area around the pond and selected a spot on a small hill that faced south. That would be their building site. Since they couldn't build until the spring thaw, they built a snow igloo to stay in temporarily. Then they went back to the sled down on the shore and brought it up the hill to their new home. This was almost starting to seem like a fun adventure.

The next day he reminded her that they would again need a way to keep meat cold through the brief summer. They had built an icehouse the previous spring. Now they were experienced builders. In a few days they had enough ice to last all summer.

By then their food supply was getting low. They knew there were seals and fish near the shore. With nothing else that they needed to do before the ice began to melt, they decided to try their hand at hunting seals at their breathing holes. He had read about how the Eskimos caught seals, and he was sure he could do the same. She had nothing else to do for the time being, and she didn't like having to stay at the igloo all alone. She didn't want to watch him kill a seal, but she knew it was necessary.

As they stood by a breathing hole, she wanted to talk. He reminded her that they had to be completely quiet so as not to frighten the seals away. He had said a seal usually comes up for air after about twenty minutes, but they waited an hour without seeing one. Finally she had to ask what was wrong. He reminded her that the seals had more than one hole. They must be using different ones. She thought that meant they should be trying a different hole. He insisted that they remain there.

"I don't understand. How can we catch a seal at a hole they are not using?"

"This hole is not frozen over. They won't let it freeze. Without air they die. We know they will have to come here soon to keep the hole open. Then we will try to catch one."

"If they have several holes, maybe they have decided to abandon this one."

"If you were a seal and your life depended on getting air, would you let a hole freeze over?"

"I'm not a seal. How would I know what a seal thinks?"

"Okay, suppose you were a blond and you needed air to stay alive, wouldn't you try to get it?"

"I am a blond, but I wouldn't try living under the ice in the first place. I'm cold enough already."

"What you need is more blubber."

"Oh great, before you wanted me to be a dog, and now you want me to be a seal. What's next, a polar bear?"

"Polar bears are great mothers."

"What about the males? Do they make great fathers?"

"Not at all. They are the ultimate deadbeat dads. They do nothing to help raise the cubs, and they would eat them if the mothers didn't protect them."

"That's awful. Remind me not to marry a polar bear."

He was about to respond when she noticed the water in the hole was moving up and down. "Why is the water moving?" she asked.

"Maybe it's a seal. Be ready with the spear."

As soon as he had spoken, a seal poked its head above water. He immediately slammed his ax down on its head. Then before it could slide back into the water, he stabbed his knife into its neck. He tried to pull it out of the hole, but it was too heavy. He instructed her to poke the spear into the belly of the seal to help pull it up. A harpoon like the Eskimos used would have worked better, but they didn't have one yet. Maybe if they could find some driftwood, they could make one. He asked for her knife.

"Why do you need my knife?"

"This is no time to ask questions. Just give me the knife."

"I don't see why you need my knife when you have your own."

"Does everything have to be an argument with you? Just give me the knife."

"Well, okay, but I don't see why you can't just tell me why you need it."

She held the spear with one hand while she pulled out the knife from the sealskin sheath. He grabbed it and stabbed it into the other side of the seal's neck. Now he had a better grip. He told her to help as he yanked the seal out of the breathing hole. It weighed close to two hundred pounds. When they got it up on the ice, they examined it.

"Now do you see why I needed your knife?"

"Yes, but you could have told me."

"We didn't have time for a lengthy explanation. Since our knives are made of bones, they are not as strong as ones made of steel. I wish we had a hakapik."

"Okay, I know you used that word so that I would have to ask what it means. Since you are so eager to show off, go ahead and tell me what it is."

"It is quite simple really. As the name suggests, it is a pick. The difference is that one side of it is a hammer. The sealer uses the hammer side to hit the seal on the head, and then he uses the pick to move the carcass."

He made sure the seal was dead, and then they tied their ropes onto it and dragged it to the ice storage. There they left most of the meat and blubber and took the rest of it up the hill to their igloo. After eating their fill, they rested a while. As she looked at the sealskin, she noticed that it was different than the ones they had killed the previous summer.

"Why does this seal seem to have a beard?"

"That's because it does."

"I can see that, but why didn't the ones we killed before have beards?"

"They were ringed seals; this one is a bearded seal. There are six species of seals in the Arctic. There are also harp seals, hooded seals, ribbon seals and spotted seals."

"I didn't know there were so many kinds of seals."

"There are a lot more than that. There are about 33 species of seals that are still living and about 50 that are extinct. There are also sea lions and walruses, which are related to the seals."

"I didn't know seals were so big."

"This is a small one. Bearded seals can be 800 pounds."

"Wow, are they the biggest seals?"

"No, they are probably the biggest species we will see, but hooded seals can be 10 feet long and weigh 880 pounds. They are the biggest in the Arctic, but the male southern elephant seal typically weighs 6600 pounds."

"6600 pounds! That's as big as a whale."

"Actually, it is bigger than the beluga whale or the narwhal, which are the only ones we are likely to see, but the blue whale weighs 200 tons."

"Okay, forget the whales. It looks like we will have plenty to eat for a while. What about our new home?"

"Temperatures will be rising above freezing in a few days. Then our igloo will melt. We will have to stay in a tent for a while until the tundra thaws enough so that we can start cutting the sod for our winter house."

"Well, okay, but I just want you to know that if I have to live in a tent during construction, I want a cathedral ceiling, bay windows and central air."

"I can assure you that there will be some air in the center of the house." He thought for a moment and then added, "If we can find some driftwood, maybe we can make a window. Since it will face the bay, I guess you could call it a bay window."

"Such luxury! What about fire?"

"I have been thinking about that too. We have seal oil now. Maybe sometime we can start a fire."

"Do you really think that is possible?"

"I think so. For now we need to focus on our new home."

A few days later the snow began to melt. They would need a tent to stay in for a while. As the snow disappeared from the shore, they went along the edge of the water to see if they could find any wood. Here and there they found a few pieces. It took a lot of time, but in a few days they had a respectable pile for their construction needs. By the end of May their igloo caved in. Of course, they had expected that. They selected a few pieces of wood that seemed appropriate for their purpose and constructed a tent with the sealskins.

Now the sun was shining all day and all night. As the month of June came, the sod began to thaw. This was what they had been waiting for. They began cutting blocks for their new home. Little by little the walls rose. They were indeed able to form a window from the driftwood. When the walls were high enough, he remembered what she had said about a cathedral ceiling. Maybe they would have enough wood to make a roof. There was grass they could use for thatch. He thought about it and decided it should work. In a few days they had a suitable one room house.

Their only entrance was through the window, but that seemed like a minor inconvenience. It was only mid June. There was plenty of time before winter. Since they had adequate food, they decided to make a second room. It was much like the first and only took a week to build. Now they each had a room.

Then they decided to make a longer trek along the shore to see if there was any more wood. They found some and gathered enough to make a real doorway. They had adequate food and clothing, and now they even had the best house they had seen in nearly two years. How could life get any better?

Chapter 29 Fire

She had said at one time that if she could just have fire, she could be content. With all their other needs satisfied for the time being, he turned his attention to making a seal oil lamp. He had read about how the Eskimos made their lamps. Could he do it? It seemed like it should be possible. After all, the lamp was the most important article in the Eskimo home. Nearly every family had one. Again she could tell he was thinking about something.

"What is it this time? I can almost see the wheels turning in that thick head of yours."

"You had better be nice, or I will keep the heat in my own room."

"What heat? We don't have any fire or any way to make it."

"It is true we don't have any fire, but it is not necessarily true that we can't make any."

"Don't tell me you have had a lighter in your pocket all this time."

"Not exactly."

"What is that supposed to mean? Will you stop toying with me!"

"If we had a lighter, it would not have done us much good before now."

"What do you mean?"

"Well, first of all, we would need something for fuel. We can't burn wood because there is very little of it, and it must be saved for more important things."

"Yes, but you said we can use seal oil. We have plenty of that now, and I hate eating it."

"Blubber is an ideal food for active people in very cold weather. It has a high calorie content."

"That may be true, but it tastes yucky."

"When a person is trying to stay alive, taste is not the most important consideration."

"We are not in danger of starving now, so how about lighting up some seal oil. I'm still cold."

"If you were a brunette, maybe you could understand that we need something to put the oil in to burn it."

"So it's back to that again. What does it take to get a little respect from you?"

"Have you considered dyeing your hair?"

"I've considered someone dying, and with great violence."

"Okay, settle down. I was just joking."

"I don't find it funny at all. What about the fire? What can we put the seal oil in to burn it?"

"A seal oil lamp."

"Well, Mr. Wizard, in case you haven't noticed, we don't have one."

"So what does that tell you?"

"Will you stop that? Just tell me what your plan is."

"Logically, the options are to buy one or make one."

"We both know that we can't buy anything."

"Why didn't I think to bring more cash with me?"

"You just love to irritate me, don't you? You know there is no one here to buy anything from. Since we can't buy a lamp, we will have to make one. What do we need to make it?"

"Soapstone."

"There you go again with your one-word answers. Explain yourself."

"Soapstone is the best choice for a seal oil lamp. Of course, any stone will do. It needs to be elliptical or half-moon shape. Normally the lamps were a couple feet long and about half as wide. They need to be hollowed out to hold the oil, and they are three or four inches deep."

She thought for a minute. What he described sounded reasonable. They should be able to make it. She hesitated to ask any more questions because he always made her appear ignorant, but her curiosity made her overcome her hesitation.

"Okay, so if we make a lamp like you described, how do we make it work?"

"First, we fill it with blubber and level it off. Then we need something for a wick. Cotton grass is something that grows in the Arctic that works well. Moss is another common wick. Then we just need to light it and have the women watch it continually to keep it from smoking too much."

"I'm the only woman here."

"Bingo."

"I suppose you are going to tell me that tending the lamp is woman's work."

"That's right. The men spend most of their time hunting and fishing. They can't be home all the time to watch the lamps."

"Well, okay, but there is just one problem. How do we light it?"

"Fire."

"Another one-word answer. The whole problem in the first place is that we don't have any fire."

"Then let's make some."

"How?"

"That's a one-word question."

"Okay, try this: How do we start a fire without matches?"

"That's simple enough. Just pull out your smart phone, say, 'Hey, Siri.' and then ask, 'How can I start a fire without matches?'"

"I think my battery is low."

"It is lucky for you that I am here."

"I can barely contain my joy. Now stop playing around and tell me how we can start a fire."

"There are many methods of starting fire. Friction is one of the most common. We could also focus sunlight. Then there is the flint and steel method. Those are the choices we have. Sugar and potassium permanganate will start a fire rather quickly. So will a battery and steel wool, but of course we don't have them."

"I can't believe I forgot to bring along my potassium per— whatever."

"Permanganate"

"Okay, but I see you don't have any either."

"Right you are. So let's use what we do have."

"I'm glad it's not possible to start a fire with urine or you would want to try that."

"Actually, it is possible to start a fire with urine."

"Now wait a minute. Urine is mostly water, and water is a product of combustion. It can't be used to start a fire. It could only be used to put out a fire."

"No, it is possible to start a fire with urine, but ordinary water works just as well."

"I know I am going to regret asking this, but how can you use water to start a fire?"

"It is simple. Just put it into a water bottle and use the bottle to focus the sunlight just like a magnifying glass."

"So then, if you are just using the bottle to focus the sunlight, why would you consider using urine?"

"You might be in the desert and not have any water."

"We're not in a desert, and we don't have a water bottle."

"We don't need a water bottle."

"You just said we would have to put the water in a bottle. Make up your mind."

"Since it is cold here, we could form a piece of ice into a magnifying glass."

"So now you think you can use ice to make a fire."

"You can, but I think it would be easier to just use a lighter."

"Okay, Mr. Pyromaniac, do you have a lighter?"

"Sorta."

"What kind of answer is that?"

"Well, a lighter uses a flint to make a spark. We have flint."

"But we don't have any butane."

"No, but the tundra does emit methane."

"Are you saying we can gather methane gas and ignite it with a flint?"

"No, I just said a flint can make a spark, and the tundra emits methane."

"Will you stop beating around the bush, and tell me how you plan to start a fire?"

"I suggest we try rubbing two sticks together."

"I thought you said wood is too valuable to use for fire."

"It is."

"But you just said we should rub two sticks together."

"That's right."

"If you don't stop trying to irritate me, you won't need anything to start a fire because I am getting so hot under the collar, I am about to burst into flames."

"You are the one who is always complaining about being cold."

"I am cold. I am also hot."

"Spoken as a true blond."

"Where are those two sticks? I need them."

"Would you rather beat me or have a fire?"

"I want a fire. If you think you can start one just by rubbing sticks together, then stop talking and get on with it."

"It is not quite that simple."

"Why doesn't that surprise me? So then, how can we start a fire?"

"Using the friction method, there are three ways: the hand drill, the bow drill and the fire plow. The bow drill usually works best. It can normally create enough heat to start a fire in about fifteen minutes."

"What's a bow drill?"

"It is a lot like a bow used to shoot arrows, but it is smaller. All we have to do is wrap the string around a wooden rod and pull it back and forth to make the rod rotate. The end of the rod is in a hole with combustible material. When the friction produces enough heat, an ember starts to burn. We transfer the ember to some dry grass and blow gently on it until it bursts into flame."

She thought about his explanation. It sounded feasible. "Okay," she said. "I really would like to have a fire. Let's try it."

It took a couple days to find a suitable stone and to fashion it into a lamp, but they were successful. Then they made a bow drill and gathered dry grass and sticks to get the fire going when they used the drill. The plan worked. They got a fire started and then transferred a burning stick to the moss wick in the oil filled lamp. For the first time in nearly two years they had fire.

Chapter 30 Matrimonial Bliss

Their lives now seemed complete. They had plenty of meat, running water, clothes and a house that was a major improvement over the pile of rocks with which they had started. Best of all they could finally cook their food. It didn't take long for her to learn to tend the lamp. The moss wick was not ideal, but it did the job. She was able to keep it from smoking by frequent trimming.

The sun was shining all night now. Temperatures were in the fifties. One day while he was out fishing, she went out by the pool and sat down. It was a little after noon, and the sky was clear for a change. Normally there was a lot of fog. As she sat there, suddenly she realized that she was warm. That had not happened before. Even the previous summer she had never really felt warm. She removed her sealskin parka and pants. Then she took off her mukluks. Looking down at her dress, she noticed how yellowed and wrinkled it was. She had never had it off all the time they had been in the Arctic. It also smelled bad.

She thought to herself, "Well, I guess the pool is the closest thing we have to a Laundromat, and I don't even need any money." With that she removed the dress and put the parka back on. She washed the dress in the pool, hung it up to dry from the roof of the house, and returned to the pool. Dipping her foot into the water, she learned it was too cold for swimming, but maybe she could go wading. After splashing around a bit she stepped back out before her feet got too cold. Bending over the edge of the pool, she looked at her reflection in the still water. Her face really needed washing, and her hair was a mess. The hairs that had been cut short had grown out a couple inches. Having half her hair short and half long looked rather odd. What could she do with it? She decided to tie it in a ponytail with a piece of seal gut.

It was such a beautiful warm day, she just wanted to enjoy the sun while she waited for her dress to dry. Running back into the house, she retrieved the bear skin and laid it on the ground by the pool. Then she lay down on it and closed her eyes. The sun felt so good. Opening her eyes again, she looked around. The Arctic poppies were blooming in profusion. She looked down at the bay. There was a slight haze over the water. She could hear the stream bubbling as it descended the hill. A little way down the hill she could see some lemmings playing. They could have caught some of them to eat, but with plenty of other game from which to choose they didn't care to eat rodents. They would leave them to the Arctic foxes for now.

Closing her eyes again, she soaked in the warm sunshine. She remembered watching movies in which the celebrities lay in the sun by a pool. That was just what she was doing. She even had a genuine bear skin to lie on. Yes, life was good.

Then she thought back to the previous winter. It had been cold, and it was such hard work pulling the sled. Every day they had to build a new home. There had been no way of knowing if or when they might find a new island. Then she remembered how close they had come to being killed by polar bears. It had been terrifying.

Opening her eyes, she looked around again. It was so serene.

She closed her eyes again and thought about the coming winter when they would try to make it to the mainland. Even with all the trouble of the previous winter, they had not made it halfway to their goal. What if the bears killed them in their attempt next winter? It was fairly safe here. Maybe it would be better to just stay where they were.

Reopening her eyes, she thought how beautiful it was on this island that they had all to themselves. Not only that, but next winter they would have heat and light in their home.

Wait a minute. They wouldn't have fire if she didn't keep the lamp going. Jumping up, she ran back to the house. The fire was low, but she was able to get it going again.

He would be coming back for lunch soon. It was time to start cooking. She remembered her mother telling her that the fastest way to a man's heart is through his stomach. Could he be persuaded to stay here instead of risking everything to reach the mainland? Going to the ice storage, she selected a nice piece of seal liver. That was his favorite meat.

As soon as he entered the house, he had the impression that something was up. The meat smelled good. He noticed that she was wearing her dress without the parka. That was understandable. It was a warm day. Her hair was in a ponytail. She smiled at him and said that the meal was ready. Why was she acting so friendly?

As he ate, he noticed that she was not eating very much. Why did she keep smiling? Neither said anything until he finished his liver. Then she asked if he wanted some water. Why didn't she tell him to get it himself?

Finally, he had to ask if she had something on her mind. She hesitated and then said, "I've been thinking."

He was tempted to ask what she had to think with, but that didn't seem like a very good idea. Instead he simply asked, "What have you been thinking?"

"Well, you know what a hard time we had last winter. The bears nearly got us several times. We really don't even know where we are. We might never make it to the mainland. Here we have everything we need. In fact, now that we have fire, we have just about everything we could want. That is, we have everything we could want except family."

"Family?"

"You know…..children."

"Children? Just what are you suggesting?"

"Well, what I was thinking, that is, I mean, you know. Do you, um, do you maybe, sorta…   Do you find me…..attractive?"

"I suppose. Why?"

"Well, I was thinking maybe we could, well you know, get together."

"We've been together for nearly two years."

"You know what I mean."

"We're not married."

"Well, there is no preacher here to marry us."

"Exactly."

"So, how did the Eskimos do it?"

He was very uncomfortable with the way this conversation was going. He was glad she had asked about the marriage customs of the Eskimos. It gave him something to talk about that was a little less personal. He started, "There was often a shortage of women to marry because of the difficulty of raising children to adulthood. Sometimes the girl babies were killed at birth."

"That's horrible. Why would they do that?"

"It was a matter of survival. The men were the hunters; girls were just more mouths to feed."

"I think that is inexcusable. Why have babies if they were going to kill them?"

"They needed boys to have new hunters."

"So, if there was a shortage of girls to marry, what did they do?"

"Sometimes they would raid other villages and kidnap eligible women."

"Surely there had to be a more civilized way to get a wife."

"Yes, there were more approved ways of getting married if a couple wanted to do things properly."

"Good, tell me about gentlemen's courtship and marriage procedures."

"If a couple wanted to get married properly, the first thing to do was for the father of the groom to visit the father of the bride. They would talk about hunting and the weather and their dogs. At some point in the conversation the father of the groom would say something to the effect, 'It's too bad my son is such a bad hunter that any woman he married would probably starve to death.' That means 'My son wants to marry your daughter.' The father of the bride then needs to approve or disapprove. If the answer is no, the father of the bride says something like 'Maybe there are some eligible women in one of the villages up the coast.' If the answer is yes, he will say something like 'It is too bad my daughter is so ugly no one would ever want to marry her.'"

"Why couldn't they just ask for approval and then get a simple *yes* or *no*?"

"That would be too forward. One would not want to appear immodest."

"Okay, but what about the actual marriage?"

"As the wedding day approaches, the groom visits the tent of the bride and her family."

"I thought they lived in igloos."

"Only in the winter. Weddings take place in the summer when they are living in sealskin tents."

"Fine, let's get to the wedding ceremony."

"The groom visits with the father of the bride. They talk about hunting, fishing, dogs and so forth. It would be inappropriate to make any notice of the bride. After a few days the groom suddenly bursts into the tent unannounced. The father of the bride says, 'It looks like we have a visitor.' That is equivalent to saying 'Her mother and I do' when the preacher asks who gives the woman to be married to the man. Just like in our marriage ceremonies, the father then retires. Next the groom approaches the bride, who has stationed herself by the main tent pole that supports the tent. She kicks him in the face."

"Wait a minute. That doesn't make any sense. I thought she wanted to get married."

"She does."

"Then why would she kick him in the face?"

"It would be immodest for a girl to appear too eager.'

"Then what?"

"He tries again. She scratches his face. He keeps trying to grab her and carry her off. She keeps scratching, biting and kicking. During this whole time the mother and others are just watching and chuckling. Finally, the mother of the bride says something to the effect, 'It's no use; we poor women are doomed to forever be abused by men.' That is equivalent to the preacher saying, 'I now pronounce you man and wife.' The bride then stops fighting. The groom carries her out and throws her down on his sled. She says to the dogs, 'Shut up, you stupid dogs; don't you know we are going home?' That shows that she considers her husband's home to be her home. Then they go off on their honeymoon. As they visit the villages along the coast, the people see his bruises, and they know the pair is a happily married couple on their honeymoon."

She was stunned and didn't say anything for a minute. Then she replied, "You made that up."

"No, I didn't. I read it in a book."

"What book?'

"*Book of the Eskimos* by Peter Freuchen."

"What did he know about it?"

"He lived among the Eskimos for many years. He had an Eskimo wife."

"I suppose you are going to tell me he just grabbed her."

"That's right."

"No way."

"It's in the book. When we get back to civilization, you can read it for yourself."

"They must not have had much of a marriage."

"Actually, they were happily married for several years until she died from the Spanish flu. They had a couple of children."

Again she was silent for a time to think about what he had said. Then she replied, "Well, you had better not try grabbing me."

"Don't worry. I have no intention of doing any such thing."

She thought about it and then asked, "Are you sure you don't want to?"

"We need to stay focused on our goal. Besides, we are not Adam and Eve. There are over seven billion people in the world. You deserve more than one option to choose from."

"Well, I don't want to leave. I want to stay here.....with you."

"No, you don't."

"Yes, I do. I'll even chew hides for you."

"Look, I'm not staying here, and I am not leaving you here alone."

"What if I refuse to go?"

"If I have to, I will tie you up and drag you along."

"You're a mean bully. I hate you."

"If that is true, you certainly don't want to marry me."

"I'll marry anyone I please."

"You don't please very many people."

"Will you get out of here?" She didn't mean that, but she was angry. Things were not working out at all as she had planned.

He was glad to escape from this embarrassing situation. In a moment he was gone. She was left standing there with what was left of her piece of seal liver. In anger she threw it on the floor. Then she immediately picked it up again. In the Arctic nothing could be wasted.

She felt like a woman scorned. She had offered herself to him, and he had rejected her. In anger she promised herself that she would get even with him. However, when she tried to think how she would do that, she realized that without him she would certainly die. She remembered all the things he had done to help her stay alive for nearly two years. Maybe just a little bit of revenge would be enough. She could let the lamp get low and be late with supper. How about the silent treatment? No, that wouldn't work; he would like that. Maybe she could try talking all the time. He probably wouldn't notice any difference from the norm. Men are so unobservant. As she thought about it, she wondered if she did talk too much. She began to feel embarrassed.

Then she thought about what she had just done. She had made a fool of herself. Why had she been so forward? She knew that men don't want girls that are too pushy. What would he think of her? Would he consider her to be a woman of poor character? How would her actions affect their relationship? She tried to tell herself that she didn't care what he thought of her, but she knew that she really did want his approval. Had she ruined everything just when things were finally going well for them?

Then she realized that he really was a man of good character. Many men would have been quick to take advantage of the situation, particularly when she had indicated her willingness. She remembered all the times men had made passes at her in the restaurant. He had insulted her intelligence many times, but he had always done his best to protect her and provide for her. Instead of being angry with him, she should have respected him. Besides, her suggestion had been entirely her own idea. He had not done anything wrong.

Then she thought again about their relationship. He had made it clear that he did not consider her to be a potential spouse. What was it then? He was older than she, but not old enough to be a father figure. She finally decided that he was more like a big brother. He would protect her and care for her, but he would not take advantage of her. That was nice since she had never had a brother. As an only child she had been very close to her parents. Suddenly she realized how much she wanted to see them again. If he had taken her suggestion, she would never see them. He was right again. Why did he always have to be right?

Suddenly, she remembered that it was her job to keep the lamp burning. It was smoking and needed trimming. As she worked on it, she told herself that she would trim lamps but not chew hides. If he didn't want her to be his woman, she would let him have stiff hides. That should be revenge enough. Why was she starting to think so much like an Eskimo?

As the sun approached the north side of the house, she decided that she should start cooking something for supper. Fish would be a nice change from seal. She retrieved a big cod and began roasting it over the lamp. She was glad they had more kinds of fish here than at the first island, but she still liked cod.

Later it was well cooked, but he had not yet returned. Normally, he came back well before the sun got close to the horizon on the north side of the house. What was taking him so long? She remembered telling him to get out of there. Had he taken her seriously? That couldn't be. There was no place else for him to go. What if something had happened to him? What if she had driven him to it by what she had done? She began to be really worried. Every few minutes she looked down the hill to see if he was coming. Finally, she saw him. At first she was planning to scold him for making her worry, but that might make him want to leave again. That would be even worse.

When he got to the house, neither of them could think of what to say. She noticed he didn't have any fish with him. They both knew they had plenty and didn't need any more. She handed him the fish she had cooked without saying anything. He took it and started to eat without a word. She wanted to say something but decided not to interfere with his eating. He noticed she was not eating anything. Maybe she had eaten before he arrived. He was later than normal. She tried to think what she could say or do. Maybe he would like some water. She took the wooden cup he had whittled to the stream and filled it. When she offered it to him, he finally said thank you but that was all. He wondered why she didn't let him get his own drink like she normally did.

Finally, she just had to say something. "Did you catch any fish?"

"I caught two, but I threw them back. They were small." Actually, they were big enough to eat, but his heart was not in the fishing.

"I'm sure you will have better luck next time." That seemed like a rather useless thing to say. They were silent for a while.

Then he said, "Well, it's late. I guess I will go to bed." He started to go to his room.

"Wait."

"Yes, what is it?"

She tried to think what to say. Finally she said, "I know you must hate me."

"I don't hate you. Why would you say that?"

"I know you didn't like my suggestion earlier."

"It is understandable. It is just that we cannot be distracted from our purpose. We don't belong here. Your home is in Vancouver, and mine is in Chicago. Next spring we will make it to the mainland. Then it is just a matter of time until we are back in civilization."

"But what if we don't make it? We could be killed by bears."

"That is possible, but we have learned how to avoid them. We will have a better chance next winter than we had last. There is some risk, but we have to try."

"I know. It is just that we will be together for several months yet, and I don't want you to be mad at me."

"I won't. Let's just make the best of it while we are here. As you pointed out earlier, we have everything we need now."

Thinking about what he had said, she realized it was true. They had everything they needed. Why ruin it with interpersonal conflicts? Their time remaining on the island could be quite pleasant. There just wouldn't be any matrimonial bliss. Since she had never been married before, it should not be a problem to be unmarried now.

Chapter 31 Paradise Lost

The short Arctic summer passed quickly. The sun began dipping below the horizon again at night. For a few weeks the temperatures remained fairly mild. He spent a lot of time fishing. There were many Arctic char and flounder as well as cod. Once he saw a beluga whale, and a couple times he saw narwhals. Of course, he couldn't catch anything so big without an umiak and other helpers. He hoped to see a walrus, but he didn't.

August came and went. In late September they celebrated their second year in the Arctic. As they thought back to the day they had arrived, they remembered how desperate they had been. Their condition now was so much better it seemed like paradise. They would not need to fear hunger or cold during the coming winter, and they would even have light for the first time when it was dark all day.

They would not attempt leaving the island until March. There was no point trying to travel when the days were so short, and there would be nearly three months in the spring before the ice melted. That should be more than enough time to reach the mainland if they didn't find another island. Besides, they were quite comfortable on their big beautiful island.

In October the ocean began to freeze over again. He looked forward to hunting seals at their breathing holes when the ice was strong enough to hold him. He had managed to make a harpoon from driftwood and bones. It would work better than his spear. He had also made an extra spear. As the temperatures dropped, he was thankful for the dry grass she had gathered to line his mukluks. He could see why the Eskimos needed their women to do all the things that they would not have time to do if they were to hunt.

The sun continued to rise a few days more in November than it had at their first island. Of course, that meant that they wouldn't have to wait until the end of January to see it rise again. Having only a couple months of darkness seemed like a luxury, and now they even had a seal oil lamp to give them a little light every day. How could people be so lucky?

As they prepared for their Thanksgiving feast, she decorated the house with stones, shells and wisps of grass while he went to the ice storage to get seal liver, three kinds of fish and a snow goose. They were so fortunate to have such a wide variety of food. He even retrieved a couple of eggs they had saved since June. When he got back to the house, she had the lamp burning brightly. Normally, she had moss wicks on just one side of the oval shaped lamp, but today the wicks were all around the perimeter. That meant the oil would be used up faster, but it would be lighter and warmer in the house. They had plenty of seals. They could afford to splurge for this one day.

She usually did the cooking, but since he was not busy and they had a bigger than normal meal to prepare, he helped set the meat over the lamp. Then they both turned the food to make sure it cooked evenly. When it was ready, they sat down on the stones they used for chairs and put the food and water on the table they had made from bones and skins. They looked at the food and then at each other.

He asked, "Do you remember two years ago?"

"That is just what I was thinking. It was so cold and dark. All we had was bear meat, and it was frozen. We didn't know if we would survive the winter, and we wondered if we could ever get off that island. Now look at us. We have this big beautiful house on this big beautiful island. There is so much food, and it is cooked. It is warm, and we can even see each other."

"We certainly have a lot to be thankful for."

"Yes, but do you remember what you said we should be most thankful for?"

"We have each other."

"That's right. Neither of us would be alive if we didn't have each other." She thought for a minute and then continued, "I really do want to get back home, but I know I am going to miss all this when I do."

"Yes, I agree. You said you could be content if we had fire. Are you content?"

She thought and then answered, "I am. I really am."

"I'm glad." He wondered if they were getting too sentimental. "Unless you want to be reminded of what it was like to eat cold meat, I suggest we start eating while the meal is still hot."

They laughed and then proceeded to gorge themselves like good Eskimos.

It was dark all day now, but they didn't mind. After two years of spending most of the winter in darkness, they were used to it. Besides, they had their lamp. They had to make sure it didn't go out. It was very difficult to start a fire. They decided that he would go to bed early, and she would stay up late. That way the lamp could be attended almost all the time. They could understand why the lamp was the most important item in every Eskimo home.

When Christmas arrived, they tried to think how they could make it special. A tree was out of the question. With nothing else to do, they set their minds to finding a substitute. They had bones and hides. There was plenty of seal gut for string. He set to work building something that looked like a tree. It took time, but they had lots of that. When the basic structure was complete, they added feathers and pieces of hides to resemble pine needles. What could they use for decorations? As at Thanksgiving they had pebbles and seashells. They suspended shells from strings so that they would tinkle when they hit each other. What about icicles? That shouldn't be a problem in the Arctic when the temperature was nearly forty below zero. They put their "tree" on the opposite side of the room from the lamp. He reminded her that the Eskimos like to keep their igloos a little below freezing so that they don't melt. Of course, their home was made of sod. It wouldn't melt. He went outside by the stream and began making icicles by pouring water slowly over bones. When he had a pile of icicles, he brought them inside and suspended them from the branches of their improvised tree.

In the meantime she had been cooking their Christmas feast. Needless to say, seal liver was one of the main dishes. They also had saved one last snow goose for this special meal. After eating, they sang some Christmas carols. Then it was time for gifts. Since they were together most of the time, it was difficult to hide their efforts to make presents for each other. However, they had succeeded. She had made a new seal skin parka decorated with colorful seashells, and he had made a necklace with stones and shells. Both were delighted and surprised. Neither had really expected anything.

He remembered how the Eskimos always go overboard praising any gift that is given to them even if it is not all that great. On the other hand, the Eskimo always demeans anything he has to offer. Both of them were adopting more and more the Eskimo mindset. After thanking each other profusely for the unexpected gifts, they ate more of their feast. Then they fell silent.

After a few minutes of reflection, he spoke, "This Christmas will always be one of the most special of our lives. No matter what happens over the next few months, this will be our last Christmas in the Arctic. If all goes well, next year we will be home with our loved ones."

"What do you mean 'If all goes well'?"

"We both know that it is dangerous crossing the ice."

"That is why I wanted to stay here."

"I know, but we have to try to make it back home."

"I still want to stay, but I won't spoil this perfect day with another argument."

"I appreciate that." Then he couldn't resist a little tease. "Does that mean I can call you a dumb blond, and you won't get mad?"

"Don't press your luck, Buster."

They both laughed. This really was a wonderful Christmas. He reminded her that it would only be another three or four weeks until the sun returned.

The days passed slowly but pleasantly. Before they knew it, the sun was shining again. February was cold as they knew it would be, but they were snug in their big beautiful mansion made of sod.

The first week of March they started preparing for their long walk over the ice. It would be tedious and dangerous. He walked to the highest point around and looked in every direction. There was nothing to see but ice and snow. That was what he had expected. They began loading up their sled. Their wealth had increased so much that they would have to leave most of it behind. The main things they needed were meat, weapons and, of course, their precious lamp. It would be difficult to keep it burning, but they would make sure they did.

The second week of March they started out. When they were a few hundred feet away from the shore, she looked back and began to cry. They were leaving their Arctic paradise.

Chapter 32 The Long Trek

As they had done the previous winter, they headed in a southeasterly direction. Their sled was even heavier than it had been last time. They wondered if they were being too extravagant taking so much with them. The main thing they had was seal meat and blubber. They would need food for two or three months if they didn't find another island, and they didn't want to take any chance of letting their lamp go out. Even though it was well below zero, they had adequate clothes to keep from freezing. The main thing they had besides food and blubber was the weapons they had made. As they strained to pull the sled, she asked him, "Do you think we should have dismantled the roof of our house to save the wood?"

"I thought about that, but we have a lot of weight to pull already. If we make it to the mainland, there should be more wood."

"Do trees grow there?"

"Not on the shore. The tree line is a couple hundred miles south of the ocean. Actually it varies quite a bit depending on the longitude. In Alaska it is almost to the sea, but further east it reaches almost to the south end of Hudson Bay. Then it goes back to northern Quebec."

"Does that mean we won't have any wood when we get to the mainland?"

"There should be driftwood."

"I hope so."

They were silent again as they put all their effort into pulling the sled. By the time the sun began to set, they were exhausted. The island was still clearly visible, but they welcomed the chance to stop and begin again to make their daily house of snow. At least this year they had their lamp.

After the igloo was built they went inside and added blubber to the lamp. Then they cooked a couple pieces of seal meat. It was nice to have heat, light and cooked food. He thought she should be satisfied since they were so much better off than the previous winter. He asked her, "Don't you think this is nice and cozy?"

"It is better than last year, but I still wish we were back home."

"Do you mean Vancouver?"

"No, I mean on our island, but Vancouver would be nice too."

"Does that mean you consider the island to be home?"

The question made her think. He was right; she had come to think of their sod house as home. It was simple, but it was a big improvement over the rock shelter they had started with. All the time they had lived there they had had enough to eat. They had finally been able to start a fire. She missed the little stream beside it. They had left just that morning, but she was already feeling homesick.

Then she thought about her parents. Her childhood had been happy enough, but when she became an adult, she wanted some adventure. Why hadn't she been content with what she had? Chicago had been fun at first, but then this nightmare had happened. Now she was wanting to stay at a little hut made of dirt. It must be that what it takes to make a person happy depends on his expectations in life.

They had discussed the matter before, but she had to ask again, "Do you really think we can make it to the mainland? We already walked thirty miles south and didn't find anything. We walked all day and are still within sight of the island. It just seems like it will take forever even if we do make our goal."

"We can make it. I read about a couple of men who walked all the way from Siberia to northern Canada over the North Pole pulling sleds that weighed 300 pounds."

"I'm not a man."

"Are you saying you are just a wimpy woman?"

"You don't have to rub it in."

"The Eskimo women could run beside the dog sleds all day and still dance all night."

"I'm not an Eskimo."

"No, but you are progressing."

"I thought you said you prefer blonds. If Eskimo women are the ideal, then they should have blond hair."

"I guess nobody is perfect."

With that they ended their discussion and settled down to sleep. The next day they headed out again. By evening they stopped and repeated the same procedure as the first day. The island was still within view. The third day they could no longer see it when they stopped for the night. Now there was nothing but ice as far as they could see in every direction. By the end of a week they had traveled as far as they had explored the previous spring. She felt like they had not accomplished anything since they had gone that far before, but he reminded her that the thirty miles they had traveled was a tenth of the way to the mainland. At the rate they were going they would be there in nine more weeks, and they certainly should find another island first. Maybe it would be inhabited.

It was now the middle of March, and the sun was shining nearly half the day. Temperatures were still below zero. She thought it should be warmer since they were a couple hundred miles farther south than they had been a year earlier. He explained that the temperatures in the Arctic don't vary a lot from north to south. From the North Pole to the shore of the Arctic Ocean there is typically only a twenty-degree rise.

They continued their slow journey for another couple weeks. Some days they stayed in their igloo if the weather was bad. They had learned not to travel if visibility was poor. They didn't want any polar bears to sneak up on them. They hadn't seen any yet, but they were always wary.

By the first week of April they had progressed less than a hundred miles. She was discouraged by the little progress they had made, but he reminded her that they were nearly a third of the way to the mainland. Not only that, but there had to be more islands out there somewhere.

He was right. The second week of April they spotted an island to the southwest. After not seeing anything but ice for a month, the island was a welcome sight. Could there be people there? It took a day of plodding along after sighting the island to actually get to it. When they did, they made an igloo and settled down for the night.

"Do you think the island is inhabited?" she asked.

"Probably not. At this latitude it is mostly the larger islands that have people living on them. From what we can tell so far the island is smaller than the last one we stayed at."

"Does that mean we really haven't accomplished anything yet?"

"No, we have found an island. Where there is one, there may be others nearby. Even if there are none, we know this one is here. If we have to turn back later, we can return here."

"How will we know if there are other islands nearby? If we spend a week or so exploring like we did last year, we may run out of time to reach the mainland before the spring thaw."

"I agree. What I suggest is that we go tomorrow to the highest point we can see and look around. If there is no sign of other land, I think we should continue our journey."

"But what if we don't find any more land before the ice begins to thaw? We only have a month to go."

"Actually, we should have a little more than a month. Even when the temperatures rise above freezing, it takes time for all the ice to melt. As I said before, we can return here if we have to."

"Well, okay. I guess that is the thing to do." After two and a half years she had learned to trust his judgment, and she really didn't have anything better to suggest.

The next day he was going to climb to the high point of the island by himself, but she insisted on going with him. It was partly because of her curiosity and partly because she didn't want to be left alone. She promised not to slow him down.

When they reached the high point, they looked around. The island was bigger than the first island they had been on but much smaller than the one they had left. There was no other land in sight. They agreed that they had seen enough. They would continue their trek across the ice.

They returned to the igloo, gathered their things and took off again. They made sure they were heading directly southeast so that they could return to the island if it became necessary.

They continued their journey for another two weeks without incident. A few days they had to stay in their igloo because of the weather, but most days they were able to travel. It was now near the end of April. The sun was shining most of the time. They could travel as long as they had the strength to continue. They were becoming concerned that they might not find land before the thaw. Should they return to the island they had found or continue in hopes of finding land? They would soon be too far from the island to return to it before the ice began to break up.

A couple days before the first of May the decision was made for them. They spotted another island. They were relieved. If they didn't make it to the mainland, at least there was an island they could stay on. They quickened their pace and arrived on the shore well before sunset. Of course, that didn't mean a lot since the sun only dipped below the horizon for a couple hours or so. Even then there was enough twilight that they could continue walking if they really wanted to.

They were exhausted, and since the temperature was close to thawing, they decided they didn't really need an igloo for the night. The sled and seal skins made an adequate tent. They cooked some meat on their seal oil lamp, and then they lay down to rest a few hours before deciding on their next step.

When they awoke, the sun was shining. The first thing they wanted to do was to see what their new island looked like. It didn't take long to find out. It was smaller than the last one they had found. That was rather disappointing since they might have to stay there for several months.

She was frustrated. "I told you we should have stayed home. We had everything we needed there. Just look at this pathetic island. It is not much bigger than that first disgusting pile of rocks we were stuck on."

"We don't have to stay here."

"We are running out of time. The ice will start to melt in a few days."

"That is true, but we probably have two or three weeks before it begins to break up."

"We have been traveling all winter, and this is all we have been able to find. What makes you think we will find anything better in the little bit of time we have left?"

"I figure we are within a hundred miles of the mainland. We should be able to make it there in the time we have. Besides, we haven't been traveling all winter. We started the second week of March. It has been less than two months."

"It seems like we have been pulling that miserable sled forever."

"It is getting lighter."

"It doesn't seem like it to me."

"Instead of complaining let's come up with a plan."

"You mean you will come up with a plan. You never care about what I want."

"Do you have a suggestion?"

"Well, no."

"Let's be practical. We have an island here that we can use if we have to. We have a couple weeks yet before the melt. If my estimate is correct, it is only another hundred miles to the mainland. We should be able to make it there in the time we have. Let's go another week and then evaluate our situation. We can still come back here if we need to."

She thought about his suggestion. She really didn't want to stay there, but she knew it was risky if they got too far away. She replied, "I suppose I don't have any choice. You already told me you would tie me up and drag me along if I didn't do what you want."

"That's not quite what I said."

"You said you would tie me up and drag me along."

"That was when we were back home on our island."

"Well, would you abandon me here now?"

"Of course not. Let's not waste time with useless talk. It is time to get our sled and head out again."

There was nothing more to say. They returned to their sled and took down the crude tent they had slept under. Grabbing the ropes, they again headed southeast.

For the next week they tried to cover as much distance as possible. They knew their time was short. If his estimate was right, they should be within fifty miles or so of the mainland. They had not seen any more islands. They had said they would reevaluate after a week. Should they go on, or return to the little island they had found? Making the wrong decision could cost them their lives.

She asked, "Well, it has been a week. What are we going to do?"

"I don't know."

"I thought you knew everything."

"I never said that."

"Why haven't we found any more islands? You said there are over 36,000 of them."

"Have you ever looked at a map of the Arctic Ocean?"

"Of course not. Why would I?"

"You would if you were interested."

"I wasn't interested. What is so special about it anyway?"

"What is special is that there is a channel along the shore of the Arctic mainland that has few islands. I think that maybe we are in that channel. That would explain why we are not finding any more islands."

"Okay, so does that mean we are out of luck?"

"No, that means we may be getting close to our goal."

"What if you are wrong?"

"If I am wrong, we are running out of time to get back to that little island."

"Then what should we do?"

"I'm not sure."

"Don't give me that. I need you to make the right decision."

He thought for a minute. It was crucial that he make the right choice. They had to be close to the mainland, but they couldn't be sure. Returning to the island would mean another year's delay. They only had another week or two left. What should he do?

He responded, "We have a little time yet. Let's go another three days and see what we find. We have to be close."

"I hope you're right."

He hoped so too.

At the end of the three days there was still no sign of land. If they were going to return to the island, they would have to do so soon. They stopped at the end of the day and discussed the matter.

He pointed out, "If we are going to return, we have to do so now."

"Do we have any choice?"

"I have been thinking."

"Well, it is about time."

"Spare me the sarcasm. Do you remember last year when we left the sled and covered thirty miles in one day?"

"Yes."

"Let's try that again, and if there is nothing out there, we will head back."

"Okay."

They did as he suggested, and at the end of the day they spotted land in the distance. In fact, there was lots of land. It was the mainland they had been seeking for so long. Their long trek was coming to an end.

Chapter 33 Mainland

They were within sight of the mainland. Should they continue to it, or return for their sled? Temperatures were already above freezing. Within a week the ice would begin to break up. It would take a day to return, and then it would be nearly a week to get to the land they had seen. If they continued on to the land now, they might find people soon. If not, they would be all alone without food or any of their other possessions. It was a difficult decision. This time she was the one who made the choice.

"I don't want to be without my lamp. Let's go back and get it."

"It will have burned out by now."

"I know, but we lit it before. We should be able to do it again."

"Do you remember how hard it was to get a fire going?"

"Of course, but I know you can do it."

"It's nice to know you have so much confidence in my ability."

"Don't let your head explode. It is really starting to swell up."

"Enough talk. Let's get some rest and then head back."

They had walked as fast as they could all day, and they were very tired. The excitement of finding land made them eager to return to retrieve the sled, but they knew they had to rest. The sun was near the horizon, and it would only dip briefly below it. They spread the sealskin blanket they had brought on the ice and lay down for a few hours rest. When they awoke, the sun was well above the horizon again. Even though they were still tired, they wanted to get started back as soon as possible.

They left their outer snow pants and food with the blanket so that they could travel faster. Now it was a race against time. If they were not able to get the sled and its contents to the mainland before the ice started to break up, they would be in big trouble.

By the end of the day they were back at the sled, but they were also exhausted. Needless to say, the lamp had long since consumed all its oil. That was okay. The sun was shining, and it was warm. They had to eat their meat raw, but they were accustomed to that. They would have liked to start for the land right away, but after a very tiring day they could hardly walk, much less pull a sled. Reluctantly, they lay down for a few hours rest.

She awoke first. "Wake up, lazy bones. We are wasting sunlight."

He sat up. "What did you say?"

"I said that we are wasting sunlight. Let's get going."

"It is the middle of May. The sun is shining nearly all night."

"I know, but I want to get to land."

"So do I. Let's eat and then take off. I hope it doesn't get any warmer. It must be close to forty degrees."

"It does seem warm. All the time we have been here I wished it would warm up. Now I hope it doesn't."

They quickly ate some seal meat and blubber. Normally they didn't like to eat seal blubber, but they knew they would need lots of energy to pull the sled all day. As soon as they finished their breakfast, they grabbed the ropes and headed back to the spot where they had left their food and seal skin pants and blanket.

Even moving as fast as they could, it took three days to reach the location where they had spotted land. All that time the temperatures had been warm. When they arrived, they found that there was more bad news. Their camp had been visited, and it was not by humans. The meat was gone, and the thief had headed straight south toward the land. The tracks were unmistakable. It was a bear, and it had to be a full-grown male.

They certainly could not go south since the bear had gone that way. Southeast was not a good option. With the polar easterlies the bear could smell them. They didn't want to go back north, and they wouldn't have time to get back to the island before the ice broke up. That left just one choice. They would have to go southwest. It would take longer to reach land, but there was nothing else they could do.

They were tired and discouraged. Why hadn't they just walked to the mainland when they had first seen it? Maybe they could have found other people by now.

The bear was nowhere in sight. They might as well get some rest before continuing.

After a few hours of restless sleep, they started out again. At first they went west southwest so that they could put some distance between them and the bear. At least they could see the land now.

By the end of the day, they had traveled another ten miles. The mainland didn't seem any closer. They stopped to rest again.

The next day they thought that they should be far enough away from the bear to head southwest. The following day they changed direction again and made straight for the land. By evening they had covered enough distance that they thought that another day should enable them to reach their goal. Then more trouble greeted them.

They had stopped when the sun was about at the horizon to get some much-needed rest. After dozing for three or four hours, suddenly they heard what sounded like a gun shot. Could it be a hunter? Maybe their long nightmare was about over. They soon realized that they were not to be so fortunate. The sound they had heard was coming from the direction of

214

the land, but it did not come from a gun. It was the ice. The sound was followed by groaning and grinding. The ice was breaking up.

They hurriedly made their way toward the land. When they reached the location the sounds had come from, they found that their fears had been realized. There was a wide expanse of open water between them and the ice on the other side. For a minute they looked at the water with great consternation. Then she moaned, "Oh no, why didn't we head for the land sooner?"

"You are the one who wanted to go back to get your precious lamp. We could have been on the land several days ago otherwise."

"Oh sure, blame it all on me. You are the one who is supposed to know everything."

"How was I supposed to know a bear would find our food?"

"You know there are bears all over the Arctic."

"Okay, listen. Arguing won't help. We need to think of a solution to our problem."

"Well, Mr. Know-it-all, how do you think we can get to the ice on the other side of this water?"

"Maybe the crack doesn't go too far. Let's see if we can go around it."

With that they left the sled and headed in opposite directions along the edge of the ice. An hour later they returned and considered their next move. The open water went as far as they could tell in each direction. Since the bear was east of them, they decided to go west. By the end of the day they had not found any place that they could cross to the ice on the other side. They were exhausted again. After a few hours rest they started off again. Around noon they came to a place where the ice on the other side of the open water was only fifty feet or so away. They stopped to rest and think. The gap looked even larger further west.

He looked in every direction. This spot seemed to be as close as they would get to the ice on the other side. He looked at her and then said, "I think we will have to cross here."

"What? How can we cross here? We don't have a boat or a bridge."

"I have an idea. I think I can swim to the other side."

"Are you out of your mind? Don't you remember what happened last time you tried swimming in icy cold water? If I hadn't been there to rescue you, it would have been all over."

"I remember, but do you remember what happened when I fell into the seal breathing hole? It is warmer now than it was then."

"You were only in the water a few seconds that time."

"That is true, but I think I can bind my clothes tightly enough to keep the water out. Only my face should get wet."

"But what if it doesn't work, and what about me?"

"I will tie a rope around myself. If I can't swim to the other side, you can pull me back. If I make it over to the ice on the other side, you can tie the rope to the sled. I will pull it over. Then you can tie the rope to yourself, and I will pull you over."

"It sounds dangerous."

"It is, but staying here is dangerous too."

"I don't like it, but I suppose we don't have a better option."

With that, he did as he had suggested. After securing the sled, he tied his clothes as tightly as he could. When he was sure he was watertight, he wrapped a rope around his waist and made a running leap into the water. It was icy cold on his face, but the rest of him was dry. He quickly began swimming to the ice on the other side of the open water. When he got to the ice, it took a few minutes to find a spot where he could get up out of the water. When he succeeded, he looked back toward her. She was clapping her hands, but the sound was muffled by her mittens. The plan worked. She tied the rope to the sled. He was able to pull it through the water and get it up on the ice without trouble. Then it was her turn. She tied the rope around herself, but the idea of jumping into the icy cold water scared her so much that she hesitated.

He called to her, "Don't be afraid. You saw that it worked for me. All you have to do is jump in. I will pull you over. Just put your hands over your face to keep the cold water off."

"I'm afraid."

"Back up a few paces. Then run toward the water. I will pull on the rope and run on this side. You will be halfway over before you hit the water."

"I can't do it."

"If you don't, I will jerk you into the water with the rope."

"You're an insensitive bully."

"Come over here and say that."

"Okay, I will. Just make sure you pull me over as quickly as you can."

With that she backed up. When he pulled the rope tight, she took off running toward the water. Just before she got to the edge, she lost her nerve again. However, her momentum and his pull on the rope forced her to keep going. Before she hit the water, she screamed in terror. Under she went. Then she bobbed to the surface. He was pulling her as fast as he could. It was almost like water skiing. Before she knew it, he was pulling her up onto the ice. She coughed a few times because of the water that had gotten into her lungs, but soon she was okay again. They had made it.

As soon as they had checked everything over and loosened the ropes that they had tied around themselves, they headed toward the land. It was still a half mile off. They went as fast as they could because they didn't want to take a chance of another crack opening up before they reached land.

When they were almost to the shore, they found that there was another problem. The winds and tides had made a ridge of various sizes and shapes of ice along the shoreline. It took some time, but they finally found a spot where they could pull the sled over the ridge. When they succeeded, they pulled it a couple hundred feet inland. Then they collapsed from exhaustion. They had made it. They had reached the mainland at last.

Chapter 34 Home

After resting a few minutes, she said, "Well, I guess you were right."

"Right about what?"

"You said you would tie me up and drag me along."

"What are you talking about?"

"You had me all tied up, and you dragged me along through the water."

"That's not quite the same thing. Did you want me to leave you in the water? Besides, you are the one who tied the ropes around yourself to keep out the water."

"I know, but you can't deny that you had me tied up, and you were dragging me along. Wait till I tell the people back home about this."

"Maybe I should have left you in the water."

"Can't you tell I am joking? Now where are all those people you kept talking about?"

"There are only 33,000 people in all of Nunavut. It has a population density of 0.052 people per square mile."

"I thought you said they all live on the shore of the Arctic Ocean."

"That's not what I said. I said many of them live near the ocean because they get a lot of their food from the sea."

"Okay, so where is the most populous city?"

"That would be Iqaluit, which is the capital. It has a population of 7000."

"Fine, let's go there."

"We can't."

"Why not? You said that is where the most people are."

"We can't go there because it is on Baffin Island."

"Do you mean we have gone to all this trouble to reach the mainland when we should have been going to Baffin Island?"

"No, we didn't know for sure where Baffin Island is. We knew we would reach the mainland if we headed south. Now that we are here, we can just follow the coast until we find other people."

"Which direction should we go?"

"I don't know."

"You are supposed to know everything."

"I never said I knew everything. The big problem is still that we don't know our longitude. I think we passed between Victoria Island and Prince of Wales Island. Otherwise we should have found another big island. I don't think we could be east of Hudson Bay, and I don't think we could be as far west as Alaska. That means we should be somewhere on the mainland south of the Queen Maud Gulf."

"I never heard of it. What should we do now?"

"I suggest we go west, but first we should do some exploring."

"If you think we should go west, why do we need to explore?"

"If there are people just east of us, we don't want to walk days or weeks to the west. It is always good to know as much as possible about our surroundings."

"Why don't we go south?"

"I would like to go south a little way just to see what is there, but we might walk hundreds of miles before finding civilization, and we would be walking over thawing tundra. That means there would be huge swarms of mosquitoes. Also, the caribou are migrating north this time of the year."

"I would love to see caribou."

"Would you like to see the wolf packs that follow them?"

"No."

With that they rested a few hours before starting their exploration. The next two days they searched south and east. Finding nothing of interest, they decided to begin their journey west along the Arctic coast. The going was slow because the snow had melted, and it was hard pulling the sled. After a few days of slow progress, they came across a small stream. He suggested they stay there a while until the rest of the ice was gone from the ocean.

She wanted to know how that would help. He explained that it would be easier going if they could make an umiak to paddle along the coast. They had found a few pieces of driftwood, and they had enough seal skins to make the boat. Since she was tired of pulling the sled, it didn't take much to convince her. During the next two weeks they rested, made their umiak and caught fish.

The second week of June they loaded all their possessions on the crude boat and started paddling west. The going was fairly easy. Each day they stopped when the sun was nearly due north to sleep a while. Since the sun never set, it didn't really matter when they stopped, but they wanted to maintain a somewhat normal schedule.

Figure 10 Fishing from the Umiak Boat

One day as they were paddling along, they thought they heard barking. Maybe it was another pod of seals. As they got closer, they realized that the bark was from another kind of animal. It was a dog. In fact, there were several dogs. That could only mean one thing. People!

Figure 11 Dogs

They stopped paddling. He looked at her, and she looked back at him.

For nearly three years they had done everything they could to find other people, and now they had succeeded. The enormity of the event left them speechless. At first they were almost afraid to go on, but then they laughed and started paddling as fast as they could.

Rounding a bend, they saw that it was in fact an Eskimo village. Running the umiak aground, they jumped out and ran toward it. A couple of women saw them coming and walked out to meet them. The older one said something they couldn't understand.

"What did she say?"

"I don't know."

"Don't they speak English?"

"Seventy percent of the residents of Nunavut speak Inukitut as their main language. I will try to communicate with them."

With that he addressed the old woman, "Do you speak English?"

"Ah, English, yes. Speak some. Who you?"

"We are from up north. We need help to get back home. Do you understand?"

"You white. Why up north? No matter, we help."

Figure 12 Him and Her Meet an Eskimo

With that she pulled out her cell phone and said something they couldn't understand. Then she said to them, "Men come. They help."

"How do they have cell phones out here in the middle of nowhere?"

"Nearly all the Eskimos have Internet now thanks to the satellites."

"I can't believe it. From totally primitive to the latest technology in a few minutes time."

"We'll be home in no time at all."

Actually, it would be even sooner than he thought.

As they approached the village, they could hear two different motors. One was from a boat that was nearly at the shore by the village. The other was from an airplane that was just coming into view. She cringed, remembering the last time she had seen a seaplane.

They went directly to the boat. The man who seemed to be in charge jumped out and talked to the old woman. They couldn't understand what the two natives were saying. Would there be a communication problem? Then the man approached them.

"I understand you have been up north and need help getting back home. We would like to invite you to stay and visit, but I'm afraid we have an emergency on our hands. A child is sick and needs to go to Yellowknife at once. That is why the plane is coming. There is just room for two more people on it. Can you leave immediately?"

"Thank you very much. Yes, we can leave any time. How is it that you speak English so well?"

"I attended the University College of the North in northern Manitoba."

"Why did you return here if you have a university degree?"

He gave them a strange look and then said, "Just look around. The Inuit are lucky to be able to live in the most beautiful part of the world."

They were tempted to disagree with his opinion, but they didn't want to seem rude. He guessed what they were thinking.

"I suppose it makes a difference what a person is used to."

With that the plane touched down on the water near them. It coasted to the land. The parents of the sick child immediately put him on the plane. The man they had just talked with approached the pilot and exchanged a few words. Then he motioned to them to get on the plane quickly. They thanked him and told him the villagers were welcome to everything on the umiak. Then the pilot told them to hurry. In another couple minutes they were in the air.

In a couple hours they were at Kugluktuk. There they boarded a flight to Yellowknife. In two more hours they were landing at the airport. It was a five-minute taxi ride to town. Of course, the first priority was to get the child to the Stanton Territorial Hospital. When they were sure he was in good hands, they returned to the airport to book flights back home. Fortunately he remembered his credit card information. His flight would leave at 11:00 a.m. the next day, and hers would leave at 3:00 p.m.

After making a few phone calls, they next went to the RCMP headquarters. After explaining their situation, one call to the Chicago police eliminated any concern they might have with the crime boss. He would be quick to take a plea bargain to avoid extradition to any of the death penalty states that wanted him so badly.

Next they needed a place to stay for the night. With over forty hotels to choose from it wasn't hard to find one. They approached the desk clerk.

"We need accommodations for the night."

"Welcome to our hotel. Will that be one room or two?"

"Two."

"Two?" she asked. "Oh, yes. We are back in civilization again. We need to be concerned about propriety. It's just that it's been so long. Well, you know what I mean."

"I understand. It has been a long time. I'm sure you are as anxious as I am to get a shower and then sleep in a nice comfortable bed for a change."

They made arrangements to meet for breakfast at 9:00 in the hotel lounge and went to their rooms.

They both slept soundly for a few hours. Then she was too excited to sleep any longer. Rising early, she went down to the front desk and asked where she could buy clothes and get her hair done. The clerk told her about a beauty parlor that opened early. Most stores didn't open until 9:00 or 9:30, but there was a Walmart that opened at 7:00. She went there and bought some clothes and then went to the beauty parlor. The hair stylist wondered why half her hair was so much shorter than the rest. It took a few minutes to explain. Then she asked if she wanted it all cut to the same length or not. She said she liked her hair and didn't want it all short. They finally agreed on a hairdo that swirled her hair around so that it was not possible to tell that some of it was much shorter.

Then it was time for the breakfast rendezvous. She arrived first and started to look through the menu. Then a strange looking man approached her.

"You are looking well this morning."

If there was anything she didn't want, it was some fresh guy making a play for her. Wait. That voice sounded familiar. She looked more closely.

"Oh, I didn't recognize you without your beard. Where did you get the new clothes?"

"Walmart."

"I was just there too."

"Our time is very short. I've called for a taxi. I need to get to the airport in a half hour. Let's order right away."

"I want anything but meat."

"That's not wise. I read about a missionary who lived with the Eskimos for a long time. When he returned home for a while, he ate a more vegetarian diet. It made him sick because his digestive system was adjusted to a meat diet. You should transition slowly to vegetables and grains. I recommend sausage and eggs with maybe hash browns and orange juice."

"Yes, master."

"Will you stop that?"

She thought a minute after ordering. Then she asked, "Do you really think I am a dumb blond?"

"I think you are a beautiful blond."

She blushed. He continued, "Remember when we were back up north and you were concerned about your appearance? I told you it was only temporary. Look at you now. With a shower, a new hairdo, and nice clothes, you look great."

"Thank you."

The breakfast order arrived. They ate quickly and in silence. When they finished, she tried to think of what to say. This was all happening too fast. This time yesterday they hadn't seen another soul in nearly three years. Now they were in the middle of a modern city.

She asked, "Will I see you again?"

"I would think you had seen all of me you would want in ten lifetimes."

"It's not funny. After all we have been through together, how can you just say goodbye and walk out of my life?"

"As you know, I write for a living. I think our experience would make a good subject for a book. After we get settled, maybe we could get together and collaborate on it. Would you like to come to Chicago?"

"Never!"

"Okay, maybe I could come to Vancouver or we could meet here. I like Yellowknife."

With that the taxi driver arrived and appeared impatient.

"I see my ride is here. I really must go. This is rather abrupt, but it can't be helped. My wife is waiting for me at the airport."

He stood up and turned to leave. She called after him, "Goodbye, Reggie."

The End

Index of Illustrations

By Olivia Kinsey

Olivia Kinsey is the young daughter of Nathaniel and Shannon Kinsey and the granddaughter of the author, Gerald Kinsey. She is homeschooled, a very bright girl, and achieves great grades. She loves to draw, snowboard and play soccer. Olivia has six siblings and a dog named Thor. Her maternal grandmother also is gifted in art so she comes by it naturally.